LOVE IN THE MIST

1883. Charlotte Trent has secured a post as companion to Lina, seventeen-year-old daughter of the handsome Richard Roseby, at Middlepark in Devon, and has promptly fallen in love with her employer. But not everything is quite as it seems at Middlepark ... When Charlotte finds a bundle of old love letters hidden in her room she wonders who is Madeline? And the mysterious Anna? And what are Richard's true feelings towards the lovely, and recently widowed, Verity Hawksworth?

ROSEMARY A. SMITH

LOVE IN THE MIST

Complete and Unabridged

LINFORD
Leicester

First published in Great Britain in 2009

First Linford Edition
published 2010

British Library CIP Data

Smith, Rosemary A.
  Love in the mist. - -
  (Linford romance library)
  1. Love stories.
  2. Large type books.
  I. Title II. Series
  823.9'2–dc22

  ISBN 978–1–44480–112–5

Published by
F. A. Thorpe (Publishing)
Anstey, Leicestershire

Set by Words & Graphics Ltd.
Anstey, Leicestershire
Printed and bound in Great Britain by
T. J. International Ltd., Padstow, Cornwall

This book is printed on acid-free paper

For my beautiful daughters
Paula Kellaway and Heidi Kittle,
not forgetting my lovely
stepdaughter Sonia Farrant.
Without your love and friendship
I would be nothing.

1

It was the second time I'd seen the apparition while brushing my hair in front of the dressing table mirror, preparing for the evening meal, and when I turned around there was nothing there. The grey lady, as I called her, was a flimsy vision of a young woman in a grey morning dress, so unlike the style of clothes we wore now that I imagined it had been a fashion from some time in the past.

The young woman had blonde hair, drawn back off her face and she had, on both occasions, looked me in the eye, seeming anxious about something. As on the first occasion I had seen her, not long after arriving at Middlepark, I shrugged my shoulders and put the incident down to an over active imagination, but surely I thought, if it was my imagination I would not have seen her twice; but for now I must concentrate on getting dressed for the evening meal for Miss Lina would be tapping on my door at any moment to seek my advice on what she was wearing.

I'd obtained a post at Middlepark, a lovely house in the Devon countryside close to the sea, as companion to Miss Lina Roseby, the seventeen-year-old daughter of Richard Roseby, a widower who had interviewed me for the position here at Middlepark one fine June morning in 1883. I recalled the interview now.

'And do you think you could bring to heel my daughter and teach her the ways of a lady Miss Trent?' The darkly handsome Richard Roseby had asked me as we sat in his office on the second floor of Middlepark House. I had been somewhat distracted by the view over the beautiful gardens so had not answered straight away and when I looked at him Mr Roseby had been looking at me thoughtfully with an amused expression on his face, his hands met together in front of his perfect mouth.

'Why, yes, Sir,' I had replied somewhat stupidly, thinking all the while that any chance of gaining the position had now evaded me.

'I also think you could Miss Trent.' The handsome Richard Roseby had said without further ado. 'Could you start next Monday?'

'I could indeed, Sir.' I'd replied somewhat overcome as I really thought the interview had not faired well.

'All I ask Miss Trent, is that while you are with my daughter that you refrain from daydreaming.' Any other person would have spoken these words harshly but there was a mischievous gleam in Mr Roseby's eyes and I could see he was amused.

'I promise I'll try to do so, Sir,' I said lightly once more looking out over the large green lawns where I could now see four people playing croquet.

'Would you like to join them?' Asked my employer.

'No indeed not,' I had said.

'I'd like you to,' had been his answer, 'so you can meet your charge.'

As he spoke he walked over to the window, beckoning me to join him. As I stood next to him I realised how tall Richard Roseby was. He appeared to tower over me and, at the proximity of his nearness, I felt my heart skip a beat for he was indeed a very attractive man.

'The young woman in the lemon dress is Georgina Moor, a vain woman, intent on marrying me, and that young man about to hit the ball is her brother, Jonathon. They live at Redcliffe Manor, a short distance from here and they spend more time here than they do in their own home.'

I was to learn over the coming weeks that this was indeed true and how I would come to loathe Georgina and she, me.

'And who is the elderly gentleman?' I asked for from this distance he looked to be a pleasant kindly man.

'He is my father George, and he will

wish you to call him such.'

'So I take it the young woman in pink with the parasol is Lina,' I said.

'You are correct in that assumption Miss Trent, I'd like you to meet her now.' He said seriously. 'For it will remain to be seen if you will be able to take to each other at all.'

So Mr Roseby and I had walked together back down the staircase, the thick gold-coloured carpet soft beneath my feet, me hardly believing that I had secured the post. As I left in the Roseby's brougham some time later, looking back at the three storey building basking in the afternoon sun, the long windows gleaming, I realised how fortunate I was.

My parents had died in a storm on a crossing back from France in late February and since then I had been sewing day and night for Mrs Forester to try to earn a living, but I loathed it and now I knew I would stitch no more, except for pleasure.

There was a light knock on my door

and Lina walked in, interrupting my revelry of those important moments a few weeks ago.

'How do I look, Charlotte?' said Lina. She was a pretty young woman who lacked confidence in herself but with my help and persistence I hoped to change things, so that eventually she would marry well, which was her father's intention.

She stood before me now looking still very much the child, ringlets fell each side of her face and a soft fringe fell over her forehead, which was very much the fashion of the day. The pink dress she wore was over decorated with flounces at the v-neckline, the sleeves and the skirt both at the back and front. Fortunately we were to have a visit from the dressmaker in a day or two, when I hoped Lina would be happy to accept my suggestions of more sleek lines to accentuate her lovely figure, with round necklines for evening. The young woman had come to readily accept me as her mentor, for which I was thankful, and had insisted on including me in all the activities of the household.

'You look charming,' I told her kindly. 'But when Mrs Rivers arrives we will need to make a few changes to prepare you for your coming out ball in Exeter in September.'

While Lina looked out of the window watching the arrival of the Moors, I quickly looked back in the mirror wishing to look my best for my employer who I'd fallen madly in love with. I knew that I never dared expect that love to be reciprocated but I lived in hope.

The soft yellows of the room reflected in the mirror and once again I thought momentarily of the grey lady and wondered if I should mention it to someone, but Richard Roseby already knew I was a daydreamer and would no doubt dismiss me if he had the notion that I was not only dreaming but seeing things as well, so I decided to remove it from my mind.

The pale blue cotton dress I wore

was quite pleasing to the eye, complimenting my lustrous light brown hair which, like Lina's, fell softly over my forehead, the bulk of it drawn back into a bun at the back of my head, allowing my curling dark lashes and my grey eyes to be my most prominent feature shining out from my face.

'Are you wearing the pearls your father gave you,' I asked Lina as she walked back across the small cosy room on the third floor.

'Yes, I am,' Lina said. 'See?' she said, showing me the creamy pearls adorning her slender neck. Although I was only five years older than Lina, being just twenty-two years of age, I appeared to be much older and wiser, but then Lina had led a sheltered life here at Budleigh Salterton while I had traversed the high seas with my parents since I was a child. It had only been because of illness that I had not been with them on their last trip to France.

Lina and I walked together down the two staircases to the dining-room below, my A-line skirts clinging softly to my slender legs and brushing the carpet beneath my feet. We were a trifle late and all were assembled in the long dining-room, the silver gleaming where a ray of sunlight fell across the white damask cloth on to the richly laid table.

'I apologise for being late,' I said to Richard Roseby who was waiting to seat himself at the head of the table.

'It is but a couple of minutes, Miss Trent.' He replied amiably. 'Please be seated.' I did as I was bid and sat next to Georgina Moor, her brother opposite us next to George who on his left had Lina between him and her father. For the umpteenth time I thought how young Richard Roseby looked and wished, as I had done all these weeks, that he would call me Charlotte, but there were many things I daydreamed about which hadn't a chance of coming true. I looked at the wine-coloured wallpaper and wondered idly if it was Richard's wife who had chosen it. I'd learned that she had died of a fever when Lina was just two days old. How sad I felt for both of them; he to lose a wife and she a mother.

'I said, how are you coping with this heat?' Georgina's harsh voice drifted across to me. She was sat next to my employer and I saw him smile at my lack of interest at what was going on around me.

'I find it quite bearable as long as we stay indoors.' I told Miss Moor. 'I like to walk along the front after dinner when it is a trifle cooler.' I told her, helping myself to the potatoes George offered to me in a china serving dish.

'And do you walk with Miss Trent, Lina?' Georgina asked of her.

'No. I am usually too tired to accompany Charlotte, I don't know how she does it.' Replied Lina politely.

'But this evening daughter, we shall accompany Miss Trent on her walk, if that pleases you,' said Richard to me. My fork stopped half way to my mouth and I just looked at him. 'Well?' He said, obviously noting the bemused expression on my face.

'I would be honoured Mr Roseby for you and Lina to accompany me.' I stumbled over the words for Richard Roseby was looking at me in a strange way he had never looked at me before, or was I imagining this also, in just the same way I was sure I was imagining the grey lady visiting my room.

'We'll all go, shan't we Jonathon,' Georgina said to her brother and I realised that at no cost would she allow me to walk with Richard if she was not there as well.

'I'd prefer that the three of us went alone,' Richard said, quite unperturbed by Georgina's request to join us.

'Very well,' Miss Moor said, with more than a hint of disappointment in her voice. I smiled secretly to myself, and I looked at Georgina; she was pretty in a faded sort of way and I guessed her to be a lot older than myself. Her hair, which was brown, never shone, and her beige-coloured silk dress, although becoming, looked

11

as if it had seen better days, as did most of her clothes. I chided myself at such an uncharitable thought but I disliked her and she me, so her next words surprised me somewhat.

'I'd like you to call for tea at Redcliffe Manor one day this week Charlotte, with Lina of course. Shall we say Thursday? And of course the invitation extends to you, dear Richard.' As she spoke she looked sweetly at the object of her affection and I thought of what Richard Roseby had said the first time I had set foot in Middlepark House. 'A vain woman who is intent on marrying me.'

He wouldn't marry her surely, and I waited with baited breath for his answer. 'Apologies Georgina, but I have business to attend to this week. Another occasion perhaps.' As he spoke quite politely, I could see that Georgina was crestfallen.

'Well, you and Lina will have to come alone I suppose,' she said to me and I realised that her only intention had been to lure poor Richard to Redcliffe Manor and that she hadn't wanted to invite me at all. Well, her plan had failed to have the desired effect, I thought.

The meal over and 'goodnights' said, Lina, her father and I set off down the lane towards the seafront. It was a glorious evening, made all the more pleasant by my companions. Seagulls squawked in the distance and I could see them swooping in unison obviously following some fishing boat laden with fish. Lina went on in front of us pulling at the grass in the hedgerows as she walked. 'No Lina.' I called, 'that is certainly not seemly for a young lady,' I said kindly. 'Now walk with us.'

'Quite right,' said Richard, 'I can see you are doing a grand job with my daughter for which I thank you.'

'Thank you for your kind words, Sir,' I said.

'It is nothing more than you deserve young woman, would you . . . ' Here his voice petered off and I realised Richard Roseby was about to ask me something but I would never know what as Lina joined us.

'Is it all right for me to pick the wild flowers?' she asked.

'It is, but it would be more seemly in the daytime,' I told her. 'Maybe we could walk this way tomorrow if the weather holds.'

The weather had been beautiful since I arrived, sunny, balmy summer days that I would never forget and wondered, with some misgiving, what would become of me when Lina found a suitable beau. My despair at the thought of leaving Middlepark was too dire to contemplate.

'Miss Trent,' Richard's voice drifted across, 'daydreaming again?'

'Shall we ask her what she was dreaming about Lina?' And he laughed.

'Would that I could tell you, Sir.' I said coyly.

His face changed to one of seriousness. 'Would that you could, Miss Trent,' he said quietly.

'Here we are, the sea in all its glory,'

he said in a lighter vein and I realised that we had indeed stepped on to the promenade.

How I loved the sea, I thought and I stood still and took a deep breath inward, breathing in the tangy, salty sea air into my lungs.

'Surely that is unseemly, Charlotte,' said Lina with a smile hovering at her mouth and I realised for the first time that she had the same wicked sense of fun as her father and I flung my head back and laughed quietly, my straw bonnet nearly falling off in the process.

'Take an arm both of you,' Richard said unexpectedly, and so we walked along, all three of us, Lina and I on either side of her father. My hand trembled as I felt the smoothness of his sleeve and the strength of his forearm and I silently prayed he would not notice but, as he looked down at me, I realised he had. Our eyes met and for a brief instance my dreams had come true, but the moment was gone and I looked out over the pebbled beach and sparkling sea, with small fishing boats drawn up on the edge unloading their catch.

The large ball of fire that was the sun was starting to fall on the horizon ahead of us and I wondered if my longed-for dreams would ever come true or would I have to leave Middlepark one day — and Richard Roseby also, only time would tell.

The walk was invigorating and we returned to Middlepark with a spring in our step. Lina was tired and asked to be excused so she could go to her room, which was next to mine on the third floor. Apparently it had been the nursery in times past and Lina had slept there since she was a child. As we watched her walk up the staircase, I thought that I had best leave my employer to his own devices as much as I wished to stay with him for I was happier in his company than I had ever been in my life.

'Is it all right if I sit in the library for a while, Sir?' I asked him

'I will join you if I may,' he said, 'for I wish to find another novel to read.' So we walked together to the library, a small cosy room, lined with books of all shapes and sizes, the wall that held the fireplace, decorated in red.

When we walked in lamps were already lit on four tables scattered about the room along with comfortable brown leather armchairs, which had obviously been used lovingly. I sat in one of them, picking up a volume of poetry which lay on the table by my chair. I glanced through it while Richard perused the shelves silently for a suitable book. As I watched him, looking at his broad dependable shoulders, I then glanced down at the book I held in my hand and read the words, *It seems to me, to myself, that no man was ever before to any woman what you are to me.* The words had been written by Elizabeth Barrett to Robert Browning and how true it was, just like my feeling for Richard Roseby but he must never know, unless there came a time when he declared his love for me. I was daydreaming again, and I knew in my heart that this would never be. He came and sat in a chair opposite mine and started reading the book, which he opened, his hand strong on the cover. We sat in a companionable silence, me reading the love sonnets and every now and then glancing at Richard, sometimes he would raise his head from the book he was reading and smile at me; and so we sat until I suddenly felt weary and bid him goodnight.

'Sleep well, Charlotte,' he uttered, more absorbed in his book than me, but my heart sang for he had called me by my Christian name and I practically danced up the stairs, the sound of his voice uttering my name ringing in my ears.

By the time I reached my room the sound of it became a caress but my joy was to be short lived. Before going to my own room I looked in on Lina, tapping gently at her door in case she was asleep, I opened the door quietly and peeped into the modest sized room, everything was pink and white with a red carpet covering the floor. Lina sat propped up in bed against the pillows, her golden-coloured wavy hair loose about her shoulders, cascading down her back. She looked so young and vulnerable in a white cotton nightdress stitched with lace at the round, high neckline.

'How I enjoyed our walk this evening Charlotte,' she said quietly. 'I'd like the three of us to walk like that every evening after dinner. It was just like being a family,' she said wistfully, and I realised then how much she must have missed not having a mother.

'We will do it again soon, Lina. Now it's time to settle down for it is eleven o'clock and tomorrow we will go out to collect some pretty wild flowers from the lane.' I told her.

'I'd like that.' She said as I helped her arrange her snowy white pillows. By the time I crept from the room the young woman was already asleep.

Entering my room, I could see the lamp had been lit, no doubt by Ruby, the young maid. I had taken to her and she to me. The light fell on to the mirror as I went to remove my string of pearls, what I saw made me almost scream aloud, but I clapped my hand to my mouth not wishing any sound to escape my lips for written on the mirror in large letters in rouge from my pot were the words, *Help me.*

2

It couldn't have been a ghostly hand that had written the words I mused, so who had done it? One of the servants maybe, but why would they do it? To frighten me perhaps? Or was there someone else in the house at Middlepark who wished to alarm me? But who? Surely not Richard or Lina, this was a preposterous thought, but my next notion seemed quite feasible, Georgina? I asked myself as, with my facecloth, I rubbed hard on the mirror, erasing the two words completely.

Going over and pouring cold water from the jug into the washbasin, I washed my hands thoroughly with the soap. Erasing all of the dreaded words completely. But were they dreaded or did someone need help? This thought hadn't until now occurred to me and I lay awake for some time mulling it over in my mind. Before I fell into a restless slumber I concluded that whoever it was and for whatever reason that wouldn't be an end of it; little did I know that I would be proved to be correct in this assumption.

The next morning Lina and I were sat partaking of our toast at breakfast when, to my delight, Richard Roseby walked into the dining-room but it appeared he wasn't to join us.

'We have a visitor arriving today Lina, so you may take the day off Miss Trent,' he said directing his smile at me.

'Thank you, Mr Roseby,' I uttered, all the while wondering who the illustrious visitor could be that I wasn't invited to be part of the day.

'Enjoy your day, Miss Trent. Lina, please hurry with your breakfast. I wish to speak with you in my study.' He left the room then and as I watched his tall figure disappear through the doorway I mused as to what exactly I would wish to do with myself as it was the first time I had been left to my own devices since arriving at Middlepark.

I went to my room and donned my straw hat and gathered together a small sketch pad and pencils and a small rug for I had thought to walk alongside the River Otter and sketch whatever took my fancy; contemplating all the while what my employer and his daughter were doing.

I stepped out of the house and walked down the short driveway, observing as I did so, the glorious colours of the roses displayed across the entire front garden. The wrought iron gates were open as usual and I stepped out on to the path we had walked along yesterday evening to the beach and I thought with some pleasure of my walk with Richard and Lina, and Richard then using my Christian name in the library. With these pleasant thoughts, I practically skipped along looking at the blue sky, across which small, fluffy white clouds scudded. There will be a change in the weather soon, I thought to myself as I turned to and walked along by the river. It was quiet and still with no one else in sight, which surprised me on such a glorious day, but I was thankful that it was quiet for I was glad of the solitude. I marvelled at the way some boughs of the trees lent towards the still grey water, their tips almost touching the river, the path was clear but overgrown with grass on one side and my royal blue skirt swished against it as I walked.

To my delight I spotted a kingfisher sitting on the branch of a tree on the opposite bank, his dagger-like beak straight and majestic. As quietly as I could, I spread the small rug on the riverbank and as decorously as I could settled down with my skirts surrounding me. Picking up my pencil and sketchbook, I set to capturing on paper the beautifully coloured kingfisher with his bright blue-coloured back and orange breast; he looked dressed for a ball. I sat for some time sketching and praying the beautiful bird would not fly or dip towards the water in search of fish, but he was still and I thought how fortunate I was to be sitting on this lovely bank surrounded by nature with the blue sky above me and the sun warm on my back. So engrossed was I with my drawing that I failed to hear the step of a stranger on the path.

'You look enrapt in your sketching, Miss Trent.' The voice startled me, as well as the kingfisher who flew towards the sky. Turning around I could see it was Jonathon Moor, I made to scramble to my feet for I was in a most inappropriate position to talk to him. His hand reached out to me and willingly I took it as Jonathan helped me to my feet.

'Good day, Mr Moor, forgive me I did not hear you approach,' I apologised. I had not seen Jonathan many times before but realised in this moment that while I'd seen him I'd not really taken notice of him. The eyes which looked down on me from a tanned face were a sparkling deep blue, his fair hair curled appealingly on his

wine-coloured frock coat, which covered his broad shoulders, and I had not
realised before how tall he was,
somewhat taller than Richard, I concluded.

'I didn't mean to startle you, Miss
Trent, and my wish was not to disturb
you either but I felt I must speak to you
for I never see you alone and I thought
how pleasant it would be to talk to you,'
he said gently.

'Indeed,' I agreed, suddenly feeling
very vulnerable and alone with this
young man who was still a stranger and
yet, at the same time, I trusted him.

'Would you please do me the honour
of walking with me Miss Trent?' He
asked courteously.

'Why, yes. I would deem it an
honour,' I told him graciously.

'May I suggest we walk the way I
have just come?' Jonathan enquired.

'Yes, that would be agreeable,' I said,
starting to close my sketchbook but
Jonathan's hand fell over mine.

'Let me see,' he said quietly taking

the book from me and looking at the kingfisher I had taken so much time over and almost completed drawing.

'I have not quite finished it,' I explained stupidly for he could very obviously see that this was the case.

'It would appear I startled your subject as much as you,' he said smiling down at me. What a beautiful smile he has, I thought and then gathered myself together.

'You did indeed,' I agreed, laughing quietly, 'but I can finish it later and then colour it.' I told him.

Jonathan handed me back my sketch-book and we proceeded to walk together along the path. Every now and then a strong hand steadied me as we reached a twig or a broken bough which lay across the path in front of us. We walked for some time in a companionable silence, every now and then I looked up at the man at my side and he smiled as he looked down at me, for he was a lot taller than I.

'Do you live far from here?' I asked

of him, more as an opening for conversation than a desire to know, except that I suddenly remembered that Lina and I were to call for tea at Redcliffe Manor on the morrow. The thought sent my mind back for an instant to Middlepark and I wondered briefly how things were fairing there and whether the mysterious visitor had yet arrived.

'We are not far from my home now if you would like to walk in that direction, it is but a stone's throw away,' I heard Jonathan's voice and came back to the present.

'I would very much like to see the Manor for we are to visit there tomorrow afternoon,' I answered.

'Very well, we will need to follow this path to the right,' my companion told me and I followed him down a short path that came out on to a track in the open once more, away from the shelter of the overhanging trees and I felt the hot sun on my face. To the right of me I could hear the sea lapping on the shore and I stopped to listen lest I was mistaken.

'Is that the sea I can hear?' I asked Jonathan.

'Yes it certainly is,' he told me. 'It is just the other side of the meadow.'

'So Redcliffe Manor is close to the sea?' I questioned.

'Indeed it is. My ancestors built on the land in the seventeenth century, although many parts of the manor have been added at a later date.' He spoke with passion and pride in his voice and before long I would understand why.

We walked for a few more yards along the track, the sun beating down on us. We then reached tall gates set into a high wall, which were open as if in greeting and we walked together up a long path sheltered from the sun by poplar trees lining each side of the driveway.

Suddenly and without warning we stepped into the open once more and I was dazzled by the scene that lay before me. A lake of green water decorated with pink and white water lilies lay to our right and ahead of me was the most magnificent building I had ever seen. The house was vast and hauntingly beautiful, its cream-coloured walls were basking in the sunlight, the building looked so still and peaceful, slumbering almost in the warmth of the sun. I could not begin to count the windows as there were so many, the sunlight playing on each and every one.

I turned to Jonathan for we had been silent while I took in the view before me. 'It is beautiful,' I said quietly and felt how a woman must feel when she instantly falls in love with a man.

'I'm more than pleased you like it so much for I can see that you are captivated by it,' Jonathan Moor said. 'Would you like to come in to see Georgina for she is at home today?' At the mention of his sister's name a cloud momentarily passed over the sun and I realised that she overshadowed her handsome brother with her domineering presence.

'If you don't mind, Sir, I'd rather not today,' I told him gently.

'Then let us walk by the lake together,' He seemed almost pleased that I decided not to see his sister and I could understand why. We walked together by the lake where I could see beautifully coloured dragonflies skimming across the water above the lilies. This place is a paradise, I thought and wondered why Georgina spent so much time at Middlepark when she had such a stately home of her own. But then, I mused, the lure of Middlepark was Richard Roseby without a doubt. With each step we took I could see the beautiful building.

'You must have many servants to keep such a vast place going,' I observed by way of conversation for I had come to realise that Jonathan Moor was a man of few words.

'No, we have but a cook and two housemaids.' His answer surprised me, little did I know then that tomorrow all would be made clear to me. We nearly traversed the lake and I could hear the sea ever closer.

'We must be near the sea now,' I commented to my companion.

'It is indeed just a short distance,' Jonathan told me. 'If we continue walking you will see how the manor got its name. 'We left the lake a short way behind us and walked across the grass that was starting to turn brown no doubt due to all the hot weather we had experienced in the past weeks. Suddenly, without warning, I could see the sea before me, the sun shining on it like crystal droplets on a necklace. As I looked back behind me I could see the grass we had walked across was on a steep incline although it had not seemed so as we walked and we were now on a cliff path.

'See,' said my companion, taking my elbow and turning me to the right, 'there is Budleigh Salterton.' And I realised that I could see the promenade in the distance with its row of hotels like dolls houses from where we stood.

'Why,' I exclaimed, 'so it is.'

'And now if you look to your left at the curve in the cliff you will see why our manor is called what it is.' Jonathan was once more passionate of manner and as I looked where he directed I could see the cliffs in question were a deep red in colour so all was revealed. 'And if you look back behind you Miss Trent you will see the manor nestling near the curve of the cliff.'

Doing as I was bid I could see that he was right, the scene was such a beautiful one I was aware of my sketchpad in my hand and wished to sit and capture the beauty of it all with my pencil but to have done so would have been unseemly and once more I thought of Middlepark and wondered again what was happening there.

Looking at my fob watch that was pinned to the bodice of my day dress I could see that it was already three o'clock.

'My goodness,' I exclaimed. 'I must start to retrace my steps.'

'Then I shall walk with you,' he offered and I was pleased to accept as I was sure I would not find my way. Before heading back to Middlepark I glanced once more at Redcliffe Manor, savouring the moment and holding the magical scene in my mind.

'You are very lucky to reside here, Mr Moor,' I said more to myself than to him. 'Very lucky indeed.'

It didn't seem to take us so long to walk back, our steps were swifter and in no time at all we were walking back along by the river. We walked in silence, what Jonathan's thoughts were I had little idea, but mine were very mixed, the river, my sketch of the kingfisher, Redcliffe Manor and the occupants of Middlepark. These thoughts were all jumbled in my head but given time they would all be unravelled and I would be able to make some sense of my mixed emotions.

One thing that I have to concede this instance was that Jonathan was a very attractive young man and from now on

I would see him for himself and would never let Georgina overshadow him.

When we reached the gates of Middlepark, Jonathan took my hand and kissed the back of it with the gentlest of kisses as if a butterfly had brushed over it and my heart skipped a beat.

'I shall look forward to seeing you on the morrow, Miss Trent,' he said, 'for I have very much enjoyed your company today.'

'And I yours,' I told him truthfully for it had certainly been an eventful day and I watched his tall figure walk back down the lane.

As I stepped into the hallway and removed my straw hat I could hear laughter coming from the slightly open door of the drawing room. It was a woman's soft laughter and I stopped wondering if it were indeed the visitor when the door suddenly opened and Lina appeared and started to run across the hallway towards me.

'Walk, don't run,' I admonished her

gently and she did as she was bid.

'Charlotte, please come and see what Miss Verity has brought me back from Paris!' she said excitedly as she took hold of my arm pulling me toward the drawing room. As I stepped into the lovely green decorated room of modest proportions I could see Richard Roseby standing by the fireplace and seated on the settle was a lovely woman with chestnut-coloured hair, swept up at the back with soft ringlets adorning her brow. I had little time to study her or to think straight as Lina led me over to a small polished table beneath the long window which was draped with soft green velvet curtains.

'Look, Charlotte. Look,' urged Lina. I could see why she was so excited, silk ribbons of all hues and colours lay on the table in a profusion of colour along with white and cream lengths of intricately woven lace, together with a colourful round pomander.

'They are lovely,' I enthused with Lina. 'But do please try to control your excitement, especially in front of others Lina,' I told her.

'Ever the dutiful companion.' I turned to Richard at the sound of his voice. I could scarce believe now that I was back at Middlepark that my day had gone so well, it was now all like a dream.

'I'm sorry, Mr Roseby, I should perhaps allow Lina some excitement for today as it is very obviously special,' I said demurely.

'Miss Trent, I would have you no other way,' Richard said smiling.

'Let me introduce you to Verity Hawksworth.' At his words the young woman rose from the settle, smoothing her pale violet-coloured skirts as she stood to greet me.

'I am most pleased to meet you, Miss Trent,' she spoke softly, 'for I have heard so much about you today.'

'Good things, I hope,' I said rather foolishly, as for once the cat seemed to have got my tongue.

'All good indeed I assure you,' the

young woman said. 'And Lina very obviously adores you.' The young woman's words held no hint of jealously or sarcasm and I warmed to her straight away, at the same time thinking as I looked at smiling Richard Roseby that my daydreaming days were finally over and I wondered idly if he adored the lovely Verity.

3

I wouldn't have found the letters if a half crown had not slipped from my hand and rolled under the bed. I had been assessing my finances with a view to buying a new gown when it had happened. It was the day after I had met Verity Hawksworth and the day Lina and I were to take tea with Georgina at Redcliffe Manor, which I was now looking forward to as I wished to see the manor close up.

I got down on my knees and looked under the bed, I could see the elusive coin wedged in the corner between the floorboards, now what was I to do I mused, for the bed would be heavy to move but I had to retrieve the coin as I couldn't afford to lose it.

Getting to my feet I lifted the top bed head and, with all my strength, moved the bed toward me so I could just squeeze behind it and rescue the half crown. I got my breath back from the exertion and then pushed myself between the bed and the wall. Struggling to kneel down, my skirts hampering me, but with grim determination I found myself on my knees. The coin was hard to budge from its resting place, I pulled really hard, the coin grasped between my fingers and to my dismay as I released the half crown the floorboard came with it and I was staring into a small gap beneath.

It was a rogue piece of floorboard that had been cut into a small square and I was just about to place it back when something in the cavity arrested my attention, now my eyes had adjusted to the light in the corner.

Reaching into the hole, my hand surrounded paper, quite a think bundle of it. Gently I removed the wad and still kneeling in the restricted corner of my room I looked down at what I'd retrieved. It was a bundle of letters, carefully tied together with a length of red silk ribbon. I carefully laid them on the floor beside me while I looked back into the gaping cavity to see if there was anything else there.

A glint of gilt twinkled up at me and once more I placed my hand down to retrieve the item, and could see on bringing it out into the light that it was a small miniature of a young man. Ensuring there was nothing else hidden beneath the floorboards, I placed the piece of polished wood back into position and swiftly got to my feet with the treasure I had uncovered, intent now on looking at my find before I was disturbed. I pushed my bed back into place with a little effort and sat down on the bedcover looking at the bundle of letters and the miniature which were now in my hand.

My first thought was how long had they been lying in secret beneath the floorboards? My second question was, who did they belong to? And my third and most important question was why had they been hidden?

My second question was answered as I pushed back the ribbon a little on the top envelope and could see written in a bold masculine hand the name Madeline. So who was she? Obviously a young woman who had occupied this room, but when? Should I pass them to Richard Roseby was my next dilemma? But a voice inside my head said an emphatic 'No.'

Looking at the miniature I could see it was of a blonde haired young man dressed in a blue jacket with a white ruffled shirt. He was handsome in a gentle way, his blond eyelashes curled over his eyes and his jaw line held no determination. The small lips were parted in a half smile, his eyes looking directly at me as if he were indeed in the room.

I made a sudden decision as I looked at my fob watch pinned to my grey day dress and could see it was nearly half past eight and I knew that Lina would soon enter the room. Quickly I hid the letters and miniature in my dressing table drawer underneath my neatly laid underwear. Just in time I thought as the door burst open to reveal Lina, dressed in a green muslin dress, a ribbon to match in her blonde hair.

'How do I look Charlotte?' She said excitedly. 'I'm so looking forward to our outing to the Manor today, for I've not been there before.'

'I also look forward to it, Lina,' I told her, going over to the dressing table mirror to check that I was tidy enough for breakfast. Thinking as I looked into the mirror of the apparition I'd thought I'd seen, wondering at the same time if it had been Madeline. This thought made me restless for I knew that I would not be able to look through the letters until much later in the day.

'You look thoughtful, Charlotte,' Lina observed.

'Goodness me, Lina, I was only deliberating as to whether to purchase a new gown for myself,' I told her lightly.

'Oh, yes,' Lina enthused. 'When the dressmaker comes tomorrow you will be able to choose the material and be measured as I will.'

'I do not think that will be possible Lina,' I said dampening her enthusiasm. 'I will probably need to take a trip to Exeter.'

'I'm sure it will be permissible for you to be measured tomorrow, in fact, I insist on it and I intend to put the matter to Papa,' she said boldly, and I realised that at last Lina was beginning to think for herself, which was a sign of progress and also a sign of her becoming a young lady in her own right and I secretly hoped that this was in some way down to my tuition.

'We shall see,' was all I said. 'What is the weather like today?' I asked, changing the subject 'For I have not had much chance to look from the window today.'

'Come and see,' Lina urged taking hold of my hand. We looked from the window together, the sky was a brilliant blue but today light grey clouds moved slowly across it. I realised that we were nearing the beginning of September and the weather was bound to change from the glorious summer I'd experienced since arriving here.

'Come Lina, we had best go down to breakfast for we are late already.'

On entering the dining room I could see Verity sat at the table sipping coffee from a white bone china cup, she looked up and smiled at us.

'Good morning, Lina — and Miss Trent,' she said in her soft voice. 'I apologise that I have finished breakfast, but Richard and I are to go on a jaunt to Exeter today for I have an appointment.'

'Do not apologise, Miss Hawksworth, for I am very lucky that a young woman in my position can breakfast with her employers.' I admitted, a slight tremor in my voice for Verity looked beautiful in a simple white cotton blouse with a frill at the neck and cuffs; a cameo brooch pinned sedately at her lovely throat. How I could ever have thought that my employer would fall for my charms, which were few against the lovely Verity's I could not imagine.

'I'm sure dear Richard is an admirable employer and very pleased for you to join them at their table, Miss Trent.'

At these words she got to her feet smoothing her black silk skirts. 'I will see you some time later then, do enjoy your trip to Redcliffe, I have not seen Georgina for some time.'

'Thank you, Verity,' Lina said as she helped herself to toast and butter. As she went to leave Verity Hawksworth turned to me and said as an afterthought, 'It is Mrs, Miss Trent, but no matter.'

She smiled her beautiful smile and then departed leaving me with a shocked expression on my face for I would have put a wager on it that Richard Roseby had introduced the lovely Verity to me as Miss Hawksworth. This put a whole new perspective on the situation and as Lina and I travelled in the open carriage to Redcliffe Manor I mulled this over, my spirits lifting.

It was chillier today and I half wished I had covered my shoulder with a shawl as Lina had had the sense to do. 'What do you think of Verity?' Lina asked me unexpectedly as we bowled along the country lane.

'She is a very lovely young woman and very much a gentlewoman,' was my answer having been caught unawares, but at the same time realising that my words were indeed true.

'It is such a pity that her husband died so young,' Lina said in a very grown up way of talking.

'Her husband died?' I said stupidly, my heart sinking once more.

'Yes, he died of consumption,' Lina told me willingly.

'And how long ago was this?' I asked with interest, trying at the same time to appear nonchalant.

'A year ago,' Lina revealed. 'Verity has been in Paris for some time staying with her friend.'

'I see,' I answered slowly, 'and how did your Father come to know Mrs

Hawksworth?' I asked tentatively, a little afraid of what the answer might be.

'She was a friend of the family or so I believe. So both she and Papa are on their own now, who knows what may happen.'

Indeed, I thought to myself and my spirits flagged again until we turned into the drive of the manor. It still held the same beauty for me but as we drew nearer to the front of the building I could see with some astonishment that the building was in a sad state of disrepair. Paint was flaking from the walls and the many windows were shrouded with cobwebs and now closer I could see that shutters on the inside were closed against the daylight.

I was even more astonished when instead of the carriage stopping at the front entrance we went on round to the side of the building where Georgina waited for us outside a small arched doorway which was set at the side of the vast building.

'Welcome to Redcliffe Manor,' were her words as she greeted us.

'Thank you for inviting us,' I replied amiably. 'The manor is vast.'

'It most certainly is,' agreed our hostess, seeming not at all perturbed by the shabbiness of her home.

Lina and I followed Georgina along a narrow passageway covered with a green-coloured almost threadbare carpet. The corridor smelt musty and little used. We were led into a huge room at the back of the house, the musty smell continued in here also in spite of a large fire, which although summertime burned in the marble grate.

There were two long maroon-coloured settles arranged around the fireplace with a beautifully carved walnut coffee table standing before them. A huge glass chandelier hung from the centre of the ceiling which was big enough to take at least a hundred candles. Two large windows with cream-coloured shutters and shabby maroon curtains were set in the wall opposite the doorway and looking to my right I could see a long polished dining table with ten high-backed chairs arranged around it.

Taking all this in in seconds, I felt some sympathy for Jonathan and Georgina for the place had obviously been opulent at some time in the past, and I set to wondering what could have happened to it.

'Please be seated,' Georgina said, indicating the settle by the fire. Lina and I did as be were bid. 'I will just summon the maid.' As she spoke Miss Moor went over to the bell pull by the fireplace and I watched her. Georgina had an hourglass figure and today she wore a light brown-coloured day gown which suited her fair colouring admirably, and as she turned towards me, looking at her face I realised it wasn't age etched there but worry and I could see why she had her sights set on Richard Roseby.

The turn of conversation substantiated this. 'You will have noted,' began Georgina as she settled herself on the other settle near the fire, 'that our home is falling down around our ears.'

'It is nonetheless a beautiful place.'

I tried to be both honest and also comforting at the same time.

'Our Father gambled his fortune away,' she continued wistfully, as much to herself as to us. 'He was a very unhappy man, but he has left us with very little. I had hoped that Jonathan would marry well, but he seems disinterested in restoring our family fortunes.'

'I'm sure one day some good luck will be yours.' I pacified her, for I could see Georgina was in an unhappy frame of mind as she twisted her handkerchief between her hands, now and then dabbing her eye with it, We were interrupted by two maids who brought in a tray with delicately cut sandwiches and fruitcake on china plates with a pot of tea. The bone china was beautiful, a rose pink in colour with a large tea pot to match and I realised that there were obviously very lovely things in this house but little money for the upkeep, and as Lina and I left some time later I felt differently about Georgina, a thing that I was to regret but little did I know it then.

As we travelled back in the carriage and watched the now slate grey clouds moving in over the sea I wondered idly where Jonathan had been whilst we had visited Redcliffe.

'Can we walk down the lane and pick some wild flowers please, Charlotte?' Lina asked so enthusiastically as we arrived back at the house that I could not deny her. I went to my room first to collect my shawl as the sun today was now and then hidden by grey clouds and the air felt chilly when for many weeks it had been pleasantly hot. I glanced briefly at the dressing table mirror, almost expecting to see another message scrawled across it but today the glass was gleaming, showing only my reflection. I went back down the two flights of steps to join Lina in the hall.

'There is a letter for you, Charlotte,' Lina told me, bringing it across. I took it gently from her wondering who could possibly be writing to me, I looked at the envelope in my hand, it was cream-coloured and of good quality. The address on the front with my name had been written in a business like way in black ink.

'Aren't you going to read it?' Lina asked with expectation.

'I'm sure it will keep until our return,' I told her, placing the letter in my reticule. 'Let us go then and see what wild flowers we can see and collect.'

We walked down the lane towards the sea; Lina today walking beside me, which was a good sign as usually she ran on ahead, her childlike ways were vanishing which caused me to think that I may not be needed much longer at Middlepark. This thought saddened me and I set to thinking what I would do when I had to leave.

I knew Richard Roseby would give

me a good recommendation; forget it for the moment I told myself and then I thought of the lovely Verity and set to wondering how her and Richard's day was fairing in Exeter.

'What is this?' Lina's question interrupted my dismal thoughts and I looked at the long stalked pink flower she was pointing to.

'It is Cranes bill,' I told her for I had a substantial knowledge of wildflowers. As I spoke Lina picked two or three and then moved onto the cowslips, while she was picking a bunch of flowers I spotted the beautiful blue of the cornflower, their blue bonnet-type flowers upturned as if worshipping the sun. At that moment my thought was that I would like my new gown to be of this colour blue, it would always remind me of my happy days at Middlepark with Lina and her father.

'I'll pick some of those,' Lina said, reaching across me and my thoughts. By now she had quite a colourful bunch of flowers, they would look lovely in a vase on the hall table.

Lina and I walked on to the promenade, I wrapped my shawl tightly around my shoulders as there was a cool breeze blowing off the sea. Today the water was a murky brown and lots of brown frothy waves chased each other to the shore. How different the scene was to the evening we had walked here with Lina's father. I could suddenly see a large black cloud hovering ever nearer to us.

'We had best get home, Lina, for I think that for the first time since my arrival here it is going to rain.' We headed back to Middlepark, walking quite swiftly and as we walked through the gates, the first large drops of rain started to fall. By the time I reached my room the rain was blowing on my windowpane and I stood looking out over the back of the house at the large oak tree which dominated this part of the garden, it's many branches were swaying in the wind which had suddenly got up since we entered the house.

Was this an omen? I mused, that things were to change and my thoughts flew to Richard. I knew that there was little hope of him ever wanting me, but surely there was no wrong in dreaming.

At this thought I smiled to myself, Mamma had always said that I was a daydreamer and I acknowledged that she was right, which led me to believe that I had imagined the young woman I had seen reflected in my mirror, but there were the letters nestling in my drawer, letter!

I suddenly remembered the letter that had arrived for me today. Swiftly I went over to my reticule which I'd lain on my bed, picking it up I retrieved the letter and looked at it once more. There was only one way to find out who had sent it and, with trembling hands I undid the envelope, slowly I unfolded the enclosed sheet of paper. As I looked at the headed paper I could see that it had come from Foster, Foster and Farrant, a firm of solicitors, at their offices in Cathedral Green, Exeter.

My hand trembled even more as I read the short letter. *Miss Charlotte Trent*, it read, *If you would please call to see the undersigned at your earliest convenience, I have some news which will be to your advantage, I look forward to meeting you, yours faithfully, Matthew Farrant.* I reread the letter several times hardly believing its content.

That night I lay in bed for some time mulling this over in my mind, Madeline's letters were quite forgotten, could this be the change I had thought might occur I mused and before I fell asleep I knew that I couldn't wait to visit the offices of Mr Farrant of Foster, Foster and Farrant, hopefully very soon, perhaps even on the morrow.

4

Next morning I rose early and dressed myself in my royal blue dress with the cream lace collar which had sleeves to the wrist adorned also with the lace which fell into a point over the back of my hand.

I then looked in the side drawer of the dressing table where I kept what little jewellery I possessed, in search of a suitable brooch to wear at the neck of my dress. Finding the oval shaped sapphire surrounded by silver filigree which had belonged to my mother I thought this would do admirably and set to pinning it to the neckline of my dress.

Always particular with my appearance, today I wished to look my best. After drawing my hair back into a chignon, leaving curls on my forehead and tendrils of hair either side of my face, I then dabbed a small amount of rouge on my cheeks to give me some colour, which served to remind me of the message left for me on the glass a few days ago. Looking in the mirror I was pleased with the finished result and felt ready to face the day.

Picking up the letter from the solicitor Matthew Farrant, I walked swiftly along to Lina's room. It was seven forty-five and I hoped with all my heart to see Mr Roseby before he went about his business, no doubt with Verity Hawksworth. Gently I tapped on Lina's door and entered to see Ruby the under maid helping my charge into a white dress printed with tiny violet flowers which was charming.

'Charlotte!' Lina exclaimed as she wriggled through the neck of the dress which then cascaded to the floor, leaving Lina's hair all awry.

'I need to speak with your father before breakfast,' I told her, 'if I am not back by eight thirty, please wait for me in the dining-room.'

'There's nothing wrong, is there?' Lina asked, concern in her voice.

'Nothing I assure you,' I told her honestly, for indeed there wasn't. 'Now let Ruby tidy your hair while I attend to my business.' I left Lina looking quite perplexed, but not as perplexed as I regarding the letter in my hand.

I ventured first to my employer's study and started to descend the flight of stairs only to run headlong into Richard at the bottom of the flight.

'Apologies Miss Trent, I was walking far too quickly, I trust I didn't startle you,' he enquired solicitously.

'No indeed you did not.' I assured him, 'I was just on my way to seek you out, if you could please spare me but a short moment of your time.'

'But of course, Miss Trent. I will make time for you always,' Richard spoke softly, commencing to walk in the direction of his study when he stopped and looked back at me. 'This sounds a serious matter for you have not sought me out before. I trust and fervently hope you aren't planning to leave us?' It was a question.

'I promise you that it is not the case, Sir,' I assured him.

'Splendid, now let us talk in my study.' So saying he led the way and as I entered the familiar room that held the aroma of beeswax, I thought momentarily of the day Richard Roseby had interviewed me in this very room. The sun had been shining in all it's glory on that day, but now rain splattered the window panes and the view out over the croquet lawn looked dark and dismal. Richard sat in his chair behind the huge desk and bade me to sit on the high-backed chair opposite him.

'Now what can I do to help you my dear? For I sense you are a damsel in distress.' His hands were together near his strong chin and I couldn't help but notice his perfect mouth. How I longed to kiss it and, at the thought, I blushed and to cover my confusion I handed my employer the letter.

'I can read it, Miss Trent?' he asked of me.

'Yes indeed. It arrived yesterday afternoon and I wish to seek your advice on the matter.' I told him, feeling much calmer now, my heart had stopped racing and my cheeks were no longer hot. I prayed that he had not noticed as I watched him unfold the letter, studying its contents.

'This seems quite straightforward,' my employer said placing the letter on the desk before him. 'It would seem you have come into some sort of inheritance, I'll be bound. How can I help?'

'I need some conveyance to take me to Exeter at the earliest convenience,' I said stumbling over the words, 'and would like to ask if you could possibly spare me the carriage for a few hours please.'

'I'll do better than that, Miss Trent, I shall accompany you if this would please you.' As he spoke the words, little did he know that this pleased me very much, to spend some time with him would be heaven,

'That is very kind of you, Mr Roseby. May I be so bold as to encroach on your kindness further please?' I asked quietly.

'Do proceed, Miss Trent. Ask anything of me and if it is within my power to assist you I will do so willingly.' Our eyes met as he spoke.

'Would you please do me the kindness of joining me in Mr Farrant's office?' I began, 'For I have never entered a solicitors domain before and find the whole prospect quite daunting.' I would like to have said to him that I would feel safe wherever he was but I knew I could not be so bold, but one day in the near future I was to remember that thought.

'Of course, I would be glad to.' He replied smiling at me. 'Shall we say one thirty for I believe you and Lina have the dressmaker coming today.'

'Apologies Mr Roseby, I had quite forgotten,' I said, suddenly realising that I was wrapped up with my own affairs and had had no thought for Lina.

'Lina has told me that you have a fancy for a new gown,' Richard said unexpectedly and I felt the colour rushing to my cheeks once more.

'This is true,' I confirmed.

'Then you have my permission to be measured for one,' he told me.

'Thank you so much, Mr Roseby. I shall of course ensure that Lina is fitted before myself.'

As I spoke I rose from my seat and Richard rose also and handed me my letter. As I opened the door to leave Richard said, 'You look charming today, Miss Trent, the colour blue suits you admirably.'

'Thank you, Sir.' I said turning to see him watching me, an unfathomable expression on his handsome face.

We were interrupted by Verity who arrived at exactly the wrong moment, 'Good morning, Miss Trent.' she said as she entered the room wearing a violet-coloured dress.

Before I closed the door I heard her

say, 'Dear Richard, you've not break-fasted yet.' And I heard no more.

As I made my way to the dining-room my thoughts were in disarray, surely I had not imagined the look on my employers face as he had told me I looked charming? No, I told myself, I did not imagine it and as I went in search of Lina my heart sang.

After breakfast, Lina and I made our way back upstairs as Mrs Rivers, the dressmaker and her young red-haired assistant Rose had arrived promptly at nine-thirty am. As we stepped into Lina's room, we could see half a dozen bales of material in lovely soft colours arranged on top of the four-poster bed. My eyes were drawn to a cornflower blue and I knew this is what I would choose.

Mrs Rivers stood by the fireplace, her hands folded in front of her over her black gown, a tape measure around her neck; the timid Rose at her side.

'Shall I measure first, or would you care to look at the materials?' she addressed the question to Lina.

'May I look at the materials first please?' Lina said, her eyes positively sparkling with excitement.

'Please do,' Mrs Rivers acknowledged, her hand indicating the bed.

'The pale pink and lemon silk, do you agree, Charlotte?' she asked me.

'I do indeed, it is a wise choice,' I told her, and while Lina was measured and discussing the style of her gowns with Mrs Rivers, I ran my hand gently over the cornflower blue poplin.

'Not too many frills,' I told Lina as I went across to see how things were progressing. 'Remember what I have said.'

'I have heeded your advice haven't I, Mrs Rivers?' As Lina spoke, I could see Rose writing down measurements with her left hand. Duly Lina and I both selected our materials and style of gowns, me all the while thinking of Richard and I knew I was doing this for him and him alone.

Walking through the hallway after

seeing Mrs Rivers and Rose together with their trappings safely in their hired carriage, Ruby the maid stopped me in my tracks.

'There is something for you on the silver salver, Miss,' she told me in her broad Devonshire dialect. Although from Topsham a few miles from here I had no accent at all so Ruby's fascinated me.

As she had indicated I went across to see what had been left for me. Picking it up I could see it was a calling card from Jonathan Moor, which brought to mind my walking with him by the river on that lovely sunny day, only two days ago, but it seemed far longer.

He'd written a message on the back of the card, *Please do me the honour of calling to see me on Monday next at 2pm. I wish to give you a tour of Redcliffe.* And it was signed with the initial 'J'.

At this moment I had things more pressing on my mind and swiftly I went up the two flights of stairs to my room to ensure my hair was tidy and to collect my cream-coloured shawl and bonnet, together with my reticule containing Matthew Farrant's letter. Before I left my room I looked in the drawer of the dressing table to ensure Madeline's letters were safe. They were indeed there, where I had placed them together with the miniature.

'I may get a chance to read you later,' I strangely said aloud, my voice seeming to echo around the otherwise silent room.

★　★　★

It was still raining steadily as Richard and I stepped into the carriage, Lina was with Verity doing some much needed mending of sheets and, as I glanced at the drawing-room window, I could see Lina waving to us. She had seemed almost pleased that her father and I were going on an outing.

As we travelled along the narrow country lanes, Richard asked me about my parents and the tragedy which had befallen them, he also asked where I had spent most of my life, and as we arrived at the built up area of Exeter and halted by the beautiful cathedral Richard laid a hand across mine and said, 'Things will fare well for you now Charlotte, I promise.'

As he spoke the words he gently squeezed my hand. *Oh, how I loved him.* The thought came unbidden and I was quite shocked by it but knew it to be true, although in truth I doubted I could ever declare it.

Richard helped me alight from the carriage and indicated that I should put my arm through his as I had done once before along the promenade. Thankfully, the rain had ceased and I experienced a contentment I had never felt before.

'Shall we step into the cathedral for a moment Miss Trent?' Richard asked looking down at me with such an endearing smile my heart leaped.

'That would be pleasant.' I agreed for

I had never been inside the cathedral before. We walked together along a path, each side of which a lawn was laid, the rain still glinting on the blades of grass.

We stood for some time looking at the magnificent front with all its carved statues, one above the other. When we stepped through the huge oak door on to the flagstones beneath our feet it seemed very dark until my eyes adjusted to the light. Many candles were lit on various altars and as we walked our footsteps resounded around the high spacious building.

Richard and I sat for a few moments on one of the pews, I knew not what he was thinking but I said a prayer for my parents and silently prayed also that this man beside me could grow to love me as I loved him and I knew I would never forget this moment.

Stepping outside into the daylight once more, a watery sun greeted us and a patch of blue sky above hung over us. We looked at each other and smiled and

Richard squeezed the hand that lay in the crook of his arm as we set off to find Foster, Foster and Farrant.

Their offices were overlooking the cathedral green and we were ushered by a young man into a room on the first floor. Matthew Farrant stood as we entered, he was young, tall, broad shouldered and fair skinned, exuding an aura of friendliness and calm.

'Please be seated Miss Trent, and yourself, Sir.' he told us, indicating two chairs opposite his desk, from where, outside of the window behind Mr Farrant I could see the tower of the cathedral. 'You received my letter Miss Trent and are no doubt wondering about the matter on which I wish to speak with you?'

'Indeed, Sir,' I agreed nervously.

'Would you like some refreshment?' he asked. 'Tea perhaps?'

'That would be most welcome,' I told the young solicitor as my mouth was parched, due, with little doubt, to my apprehension.

Tea was duly brought in on a tray and as I held the cup and saucer in my hand, sipping at the hot amber liquid I felt remarkably calm. So much so that I said to Matthew Farrant, 'I'm sure you are a busy man, Sir. I'm ready now to hear what you have to say to me.'

'Very well, Miss Trent. You had an uncle, your father's brother?' he queried.

'Yes, indeed I did, Uncle Jack, a seafaring man. We saw very little of him,' I divulged.

'Well,' continued the solicitor, looking down at the papers in front of him, 'your uncle has died and as he had no issue all his worldly goods pass to you, being the grand sum of five thousand pounds.'

At these words I nearly dropped the green cup and saucer.

Some time later when I recovered from the shock and we had dealt with all the legal aspects, I thanked Matthew Farrant as he handed me a large, blue, velvet pouch.

'What is this?' I asked, and pulling the draw string to open the pouch, I retrieved the contents and looked at it in astonishment for it was my uncle's engraved gold watch. 'Why thank you,' I said, quite overawed by the afternoon's events.

On settling ourselves in the carriage, Richard sitting opposite me on the brown leather seat watched me intently while I thought about the events of the past couple of hours that would indeed change my life as I was now a woman of means, thanks to Uncle Jack, who I had hardly known. Although I could remember his infrequent visits and the way he always took his gold pocket watch out of his jacket and say it was time he was gone for the tide would wait for no man.

'Congratulations are in order, Miss Trent,' Richard said suddenly as the rain started to patter gently on the glass. 'Is it to be a secret?'

'Indeed not,' I replied laughing. 'I have no secrets.' Except one, I mused, thinking how much I loved my employer.

'This turn of fortune will surely mean you leaving us at Middlepark,' Richard said tentatively, at the same time leaning forward in his seat and catching hold of my gloved hand.

'I have no intention of leaving,' I assured him, 'for I have grown very fond of Lina and Middlepark.'

'It pleases me to hear you say that Miss Trent.' As Richard spoke he breathed a sigh of what I felt was relief and releasing my hand he sat back and leaned against the seat once more. It warmed my heart to know that my employer did not wish me to leave.

As we travelled back to Middlepark I thought how I could now buy a thousand cornflower blue dresses, but above this wealth I would always choose Richard.

That evening as I sat in my room on the small armchair, I mulled it all over in my mind and could scarcely believe my good fortune wondering where this luck would take me; but I didn't want to go anywhere for fear of losing any chance I may have with Richard.

Suddenly I stopped daydreaming and, telling myself to be sensible, I went over to the drawer and took out Madeline's letters. Sitting back down on the chair once more, I slowly untied the red ribbon and as I picked up the first letter I wondered what else could possibly be revealed to me today.

5

Small particles of dust flew around me as I unfolded the first short missive written in a firm bold hand with black ink.

Meet me, dear heart, under the oak tree at midnight.

The oak tree I mused, going swiftly across to the window and looking out across the garden, I could see the huge oak silhouetted against the blackness of the sky and imagined Madeline and her beau, whoever he might be, meeting in the dead of night and embracing under the magnificent branches.

I was keen to see the second letter and returned quickly to my chair to open it and read, *What joy fills my heart and my waking hours since I found you Madeline. Your name itself is a caress which will tumble from my lips when next we meet. I have prior* engagements, *which irks me somewhat, for I wish to be with you, but Saturday, as arranged, my beautiful girl, when the house is silent.*

I unfolded the third letter, anxious to see how the relationship progressed, noting no date or day headed the love note so far and hesitated momentarily, suddenly feeling intrusive, but curiosity and a romantic nature pressed me to continue.

I have at last returned from London with my father. How these past two weeks have dragged by like two years away from you and of my own choosing, I would not have gone, for to be distant from you, even for a day, breaks my heart. How glad I was for the scented handkerchief you gave me sweetheart, for without it, I would have been bereft. I implore you to meet me this very night, for I can barely wait longer to hold you in my arms.

As I read the words, I sensed the urgency with which they had been written, and the utmost feeling which lay behind them. I held this letter for some time in my hand, marvelling at the manner of man who could write such words, and wishing that a certain young man would just once implore of me the same.

I placed the three letters I had read back in the drawer and counted the others. There were four left and I knew that I had to continue this very night, for I was bound up now in these clandestine meetings, and desperate to know the outcome.

Letter four read, *Now that I have declared my love for you and you for me, I feel suddenly free like a bird soaring above our oak tree against the blue of the sky. My heart feels light and my step more sure footed. How I pray you feel the same. To know you are not far from me and breath the same air is comfort to me. No longer can I keep our love a secret and at our next meeting, we must discuss in earnest what we are to do. We have visitors staying tonight, but tomorrow, when all is still, our hearts will beat together as if we are one.*

Before I continued, I laid down the letters on the arm of the chair and reached for the miniature portrait. Studying the features carefully and looking at the eyes and mouth of the young man portrayed before me I knew instinctively that this young man was not Madeline's lover.

That he had some special part in her life, that I had no doubt, a brother or father maybe, but this young man had not written the words I had been reading, of this I was certain. Picking up the letters again, I read the next one which was much more sombre in its content and as I read the sad words my heart ached.

My beloved, I have spoken to my family and it seems they would thwart us. I will not give up. It appears that our only ally is my nurse, Anna, who pledges her devotion to the woman I love, whereas my family would have you gone and no longer have you remain my sister Joanna's governess, but I will speak up for you, dear heart, never fear, all will be well. It may no longer be possible to meet beneath the oak tree and embrace beneath the moon's silvery light, but trust me, I shall think of some way that we can meet.

I will write again tomorrow. I love you and the way your golden hair gleams in the moonlight and the silver glow bathes your face, giving you the appearance of an angel, which you are without doubt. Sweet dreams Madeline, my darling, and do not despair.

I read the letter a second time and felt so much compassion for these two people I did not know. I desired to know what the outcome would be and swiftly moved on to the next folded letter which was brief.

If it is to your liking, dear heart, I have arranged a room for us at an Inn not far from here where we can talk over our future. Anna will look after you and bring you to me tomorrow *evening at eleven. Be sure to wear your hooded cloak, for I would not want your name brought into ill repute on my account.*

Trust Anna and no one else.

Did Madeline keep her tryst with her nameless beau I mused, as I refolded the letters and the final one lay in my hand. What would it reveal, that the writer of the letters was the son of this household I was in no doubt, but who and when.

No dates accompanied the love note. No initial of the writer. My only clues were Madeline, Joanna and Anna the nurse, plus the magnificent oak tree which dominated the garden, it's trunk so wide in girth that anyone could hide behind it from the prying eyes of anyone this side of the house. I got to my feet once more and looked down again at Madeline's trysting place. How often I wondered had she looked down at the oak tree and thought of her love for I was sure Madeline, as a governess, had occupied this room, else why had the letters been hidden under the floorboards.

My ears suddenly caught the sound of footsteps heading towards my room. Quickly I picked up the letters and the miniature concealing them under my garments in the drawer, just in time, as the door burst open to reveal Lina looking very flustered. 'Father wants to see you in the drawing room,' she said breathlessly, her eyes sparkling.

'Then we shall go.' As I spoke, Lina took hold of my hand and led me from my bedroom.

'Lina, what is amiss,' I said as my young charge practically pulled me along the corridor. As we entered the drawing-room I could see Richard and Verity sat on the settle together by a roaring fire. The night had gone cold and they looked so cosy together, my spirits sank.

'Lina says you wish to see me, Sir,' I spoke quietly, my eyes averted from Verity's gaze.

'Yes, Charlotte,' Richard began. 'I

wish to talk with you about the ball.' At these words, Lina clapped her hands together and danced around the room. So this was why she was so excited, they had been discussing the coming out ball.

'It is only a week away,' continued Richard. 'Did Mrs Rivers give any indication of when your dresses would arrive?' The fact that my employer had included me in this question made my heart sing.

'On Tuesday, Sir,' I replied, my face flushed.

'Excellent,' exclaimed Richard, 'and please be seated, Charlotte, for we are not on ceremony here.'

After he spoke, I sat down on the settle opposite as he had indicated.

'All four of us will travel to Exeter late afternoon,' he continued.

'Am I to go as well then, Sir?' I interrupted him. A bemused expression must have crossed my face.

'Indeed you are, Miss Trent.' As he spoke I looked him straight in the eye, not believing my good fortune.

'Now if you will excuse us, Lina and Verity, I wish to speak with Miss Trent alone.'

At Richard's words I was speechless and embarrassed. What could my employer wish to speak to me about alone? I was soon to find out.

'Have you thought anything of your good fortune today,' Richard began when Lina and Verity had left us.

'To be truthful, Mr Roseby, no, I haven't,' I answered honestly, not able to explain that Madeline's letters had been foremost on my mind and wondered once more if I should hand the letters over to my employer. Little did I know of the feeling it would cause were I to do what was in my head.

'You could buy a property, Charlotte, indeed you would be able to buy this one,' he said seriously.

'But you are surely not leaving here, Sir,' I said, aghast at the very thought. Richard must have sensed my reaction for he laughed.

'Indeed not, Miss Trent.' But did I believe that he was joking, maybe I would never know the answer to this.

'I have not given the matter any thought, Sir, but if I may, I shall ask your valued advice when I do,' I assured him.

'Does this mean you are not intending to leave us, Charlotte?'

As he asked the question, Richard leant forward on the settle, his hands clasped before him. As he looked seriously into my eyes, I didn't know what to make of his manner. Was he succumbing to my charms I asked myself, or was he not wishing to lose me as companion to his daughter.

'No, Sir. I have no intention of leaving Middlepark in the immediate future at least,' I answered, quite perplexed.

'I am pleased to hear it, Charlotte,' he said taking my hand and kissing the back of it in a gallant manner as I trembled with emotion at the unexpectedness of it all.

★　★　★

Some time later, back in my room, after goodnights had been said by all and I had settled Lina for the night, I mulled it all over in my mind and relived the conversation between myself and my employer.

Had it really happened, I mused, or was it another daydream? But I knew I had not imagined it and wondered if Richard was being a gentleman when he kissed my hand, or chivalrous.

Maybe, I would never know.

The thought of love and romance which invaded my mind at that moment led me to think of the last letter to Madeline. Quickly I went over and retrieved the bundle from my drawer and sat again in the armchair in the light of the lamp. What would the final letter reveal and should I read it or pass the whole package to my employer but the answer was that I had to know the content of the final letter or I would not rest.

Taking the letter out of the envelope, which was far more bulky than the others had been, I realised there were two letters. Swiftly I parted them and could see that the one was in a now familiar hand, the other in a hand I had not seen before. With trembling fingers I unfolded it.

The missive was brief and written in a feminine hand. Looking swiftly at the bottom of the page I saw the name, Madeline. Once more I went over to the window and drawing the curtain to one side, looked down once more on the black outline of the oak tree.

I dropped the curtain back in place and sitting down once more, read Madeline's words. *You know I am with child yet choose to ignore my plight. How could you when you so loved me. I have your letters and the flowery words you wrote only recently to remind me of it. I beseech you to help me. I am this day to move from here and stay with your nurse at her invitation. If it were not for her, what would I do?*

My pillow is wet with tears; my hand trembles as I write this and my heart is heavy. I cannot and I will not believe that you do not want this child. What is to become of me. Never again will I believe a man's loving words as I believed yours. You are a coward, Sir. Madeline.

A tear trickled down my cheek, the words so unbearably poignant and sad. The letter was obviously never sent to her beloved. Had she thought better of it not wishing to enrage him, or had the situation resolved itself happily. Now to the letter from the man who had professed his love for Madeline. I opened it and read, *Madeline, I can do nothing to help you, my family forbid it.*

He was a coward, indeed. My heart bled for Madeline and I guess the situation did not resolve itself.

My sleep was restless that night. As I tossed and turned, Madeline's words and my employer's attentiveness all turning, whirling around in my head, but finally, at daybreak, I fell into a sound sleep with the thought in mind that I would now pass the letters into Richard's hands.

6

Monday morning came with the incessant rain of the last few days continuing. I'd not seen Richard since our discussion in the drawing room a few evenings ago. He hadn't joined us for dinner either and this morning Lina had informed me that she and Verity, with her father, were going out for the day, so I had been left to my own devices and left wondering how I was going to get to Redcliffe Manor in this awful weather.

In the meantime, I reached for Madeline's letters in my drawer and re-tied them with the red ribbon. Keeping them in my hand, I walked over to the window looking down on the oak tree, it's branches now dripping with rain, leaves falling around the trunk's massive girth. Looking down at the bundle of letters in my hand, I recalled Madeline's words, 'You are a coward, Sir.' As much as I didn't want to relinquish the letters, I knew I must pass them to Richard and, with that thought in mind, I replaced them in the drawer, thinking that as regards Jonathon's invitation, if he wished me to visit, then he would have to call for me for I did not intend to get soaking wet.

Making my way to the library to find a book to amuse me, while I waited, I encountered an elderly woman on the stairs, making her way up while I descended. I don't know who was more surprised, me or the sprightly old lady, the front of her skirts bunched up in one hand while she clutched the polished banister with her other. I made to ascend back to the landing but she stopped me.

'You must be Miss Trent, Lina's companion,' she enquired.

'Indeed I am' I answered 'and you must be?' Here I stopped, a questioning note in my voice.

For some seconds she did not answer me and avoiding my question, she said,

'Is Lina in her room?'

'No, I am sorry to say, she has gone out with her father,' I replied, somewhat haughtily, for who was she to ignore my question?

'You were on your way down?' she continued.

'Yes,' I answered, feeling at a positive disadvantage as the old lady's eyes regarded me.

'I was making for the library.'

'Then I shall join you' she demanded 'and we will ask the cook to send us in some tea.'

So it was that I found myself sat in an armchair in the library, this feisty old lady sat in the chair Richard had occupied on that evening, which seemed many moons ago, her black skirts delicately arranged around her. For once, I was at a loss for words.

'I am Miss Curtis,' she spoke so suddenly, I almost jumped with alarm. As I watched her pour tea for us from a turquoise coloured china teapot, decorated with pink flowers into matching cups which stood on a silver tray.

'I'm sorry if I startled you,' she apologised, 'and also that I didn't answer your question before, but the staircase was hardly the place for introductions or a conversation.'

'Indeed this is true,' I conceded, as she handed me a cup and saucer.

'I was Lina's nurse for some years, since she was a babe in arms in fact. I could no longer look after her, my age prevented it, but you came and I visit Miss Lina from time to time,' she continued. 'So that is the part I play in this household.'

'Thank you for enlightening me,' I answered graciously, sipping at my tea. 'I apologise if I appeared rude, but I was startled to see you as I have been here all summer and not encountered you before.'

'I take it Miss Lina has not mentioned me.' As she spoke the words, Miss Curtis laughed, more to herself than to me. 'Secretive, that one, just like her father,' she observed.

I was somewhat startled at these words, for I had thought Richard Roseby to be very open and honest.

'I don't wish to undermine Lina's image, for I love her,' Miss Curtis defended the words she had spoken. 'But it is true none the less.'

'And do you wish me to keep our meeting secret?' I asked of her.

'Bless me, no child. If you wish to say we have met, so be it. It isn't to be kept a secret.'

As she spoke, the old lady laid her cup and saucer back on the tray. 'Well, I must be going,' she said looking at the fob watch pinned to the bodice of her dress. 'My nephew will be waiting for me in the pony and trap, a covered one I might add.' She laughed again and I felt that I had quite taken to this nurse of Lina's. As she went to leave, Miss Curtis turned in the doorway of the library and said

'I hope to meet with you again, my dear.' Here she hesitated then said quietly, 'Nothing is as it seems in this household, child, remember it.' With which words she was gone, leaving me somewhat perplexed at her words and with a half a cup of tea in my hand.

★ ★ ★

At two o'clock a maid informed me, as I was finishing lunch alone, that Mr Moor had called for me and he was waiting in the drawing-room. I finished my coffee and dabbed a napkin to my lips and on the way from the dining-room, looked in the large mirror on the sideboard to check my appearance before making my way to the drawing-room, smoothing my skirts as I went.

Jonathon was seated on a settle warming his hands at the fire that now burned in the large fireplace. He stood up as I entered the room. How tall he is, was my thought as I looked at him. He looked immaculate in a brown frock coat, his hair slightly damp from the rain, no doubt.

'Miss Trent,' he commenced 'I could

not let you make your way to the manor in this inclement weather, nor could I bear to not see you either, so here I am.'

'Indeed you are, Sir,' I said moving towards him, 'and I thank you for your thoughtfulness. I had wondered how I would manage to accept your invitation on such a day.'

'I have a covered pony and trap,' he continued causing me once more to think of Miss Curtis' visit this morning and her mysterious words.

'Then if you can give me five minutes to collect my coat and reticule, I will accompany you, Sir,' I told him.

Ten minutes later, with me suitably attired and sitting in the pony and trap, a blanket around my legs, which Jonathon had solicitously placed there, we were bowling along to Redcliffe Manor, the rain pattering on the roof above us, every now and then a drop falling on my straw bonnet, which caused me much amusement and my companion concern.

As we turned into the drive and I saw

Redcliffe Manor once more I took hold of Jonathon's arm. 'Please stop one moment' I implored him.

Bringing the pony to a halt, Jonathon looked across at me while I studied the beautiful building, the rain had not diminished it's appeal. How sad, I thought, that the whole place was in such state of disrepair.

'You are really smitten by our home aren't you, Miss Trent.' Jonathon's voice drifted across to me interrupting my thoughts.

'I am indeed, Sir. To say it is a place of beauty is an understatement.'

'One day I shall find the correct word to describe it and I shall draw a picture of it just for you,' I said passionately, looking the handsome young man in the eye. To my amazement, Jonathon pulled the pony and trap to a halt at the main entrance. As he helped me alight, a young man of no more than sixteen years old appeared from nowhere and led the pony away. Jonathon took my arm at the elbow and steered me towards the wide curved steps which we ascended side by side and then he opened the huge oak door and let me pass through in front of him.

We had stepped into a huge hall, flagged with black and white tiles. White sheets covered articles of furniture and I looked up at the large splendid crystal chandelier which hung majestically from the centre of the ornate ceiling. I suddenly shivered for it was cold and damp in here.

'I apologise,' Jonathon said taking hold of my arm once more, 'you are cold and I should not have brought you here on a day such as this.'

'Do not apologise, Sir,' I assured him, 'for I would not miss seeing your lovely home, whether it be snowing, raining or sunny.'

I looked at him and smiled and he smiled in return, a smile which lit up his otherwise serious countenance and then he moved me forward gently toward one of the many lovingly carved doors that led off the hall.

Before we entered the room that lay behind the first door, I stopped and looked up the wide staircase. Threadbare patterned carpet covered the treads of the stairs, but the curved banister still shone as if someone had recently polished it. Room after room on the ground floor was the same as the one before, large long windows which desperately cried out for a clean, furniture of all shapes and sizes covered with yellowing dustsheets, cobwebs forming everywhere and a chillness which distressed me as I thought what a tragedy it was.

Each step I took served to cause me to feel more at home in this place, though why I couldn't say. Upstairs corridors led to the right and left which we walked down, opening each door as we went along to peep into rooms mirroring the neglect downstairs. As we walked, rain splattered the many windows where curtains hung full of dust and smelling of must. Threadbare carpet matching the one on the staircase lay beneath our feet. We hardly spoke except for Jonathon to explain which part of the house we were in and at one point he urged me to look from the window.

'Can you see where you are, Miss Trent?' he asked of me.

'Indeed I can,' I replied as I looked down over the lake we had walked past on that glorious summer's day. Today it looked forlorn and a slight mist hung over the water where the rain continued to fall.

'It is a far different outlook to when we walked together that day,' I observed as I turned to Jonathon.

'You are so right, but one day soon the sun will shine again and remind us of that perfect day that now seems so long ago.'

He spoke as if to himself and then taking my arm we walked back along the deserted corridor and down the stairway. Instead of leading me to the main doorway, we passed through a door and I found myself in the room where Lina and I had taken tea with Georgina, but today, Jonathon's sister was nowhere in sight, although a fire burned weakly in the hearth, emitting little warmth. By now I was chilled to the bone and as if reading my thoughts, Jonathon urged me to be seated by the fire and remove my bonnet while he rang the bell and when the maid arrived, ordered us a hot drink and cake.

'Would that I could revert this house to what it was in my childhood,' Jonathon said unexpectedly, as I held the hot cup tightly in my hands to warm my numb and cold fingers.

He continued, 'The whole house was alive with warmth and gaiety then, fires blazing in the hall and every room. I used to run from room to room and along the corridors stealing into the warm kitchen for a slice of freshly baked bread and creamy butter.'

As he spoke, my companion seemed almost in a trance and unaware that I was there, but the memories of long ago must have seemed very painful to him and I mused as to how often he thought of old times, when the cobwebs no longer festooned each room and the many chandeliers sparkled with light from lit candles casting a rosy glow over the whole house.

As we rode back to Middlepark in the pony and trap, Jonathon kept turning to me and smiling. 'Have you enjoyed your trip to our stately home?' he asked with pride in his voice and I felt compassion for him, or was it something else I felt which I couldn't quite put my finger on.

I looked at him while his face was averted from me and marvelled at his strong determined jaw line and his strong hands on the reins. As I looked he turned to me and said, 'I shall live for our next meeting, Miss Trent.'

These words burned in my head as I entered the house to be met by Lina, who, as usual since Verity had arrived, was excitable and today it irked me for I wanted to be alone with my thoughts. As I entered the drawing-room with

Lina, I could see Richard and Verity sat together sipping what appeared to be champagne.

'Look at what we've bought,' said Lina with an enthusiasm I didn't feel. Scattered on the floor I could see various packages in disarray.

'See,' said Lina. 'Father bought me gloves and a pair for you as well.'

I looked down at the white silk gloves in her hands, which would fit to the elbow and realised it was the first pair I'd ever owned and I suddenly felt ungracious. 'They are exquisite, Mr Roseby, thank you so much,' I said truthfully, looking at him and Verity.

'Verity chose them,' he revealed, 'but I am pleased you like them so much. They will look very fetching, I am sure, with your new gown.'

'Try them on, please, Charlotte,' Lina urged me and I did with much laughter as they were hard to pull up my arm and suddenly I felt light hearted again as both Lina and Verity helped me.

'And tomorrow,' Lina said with

gusto, 'our dresses will arrive.'

As she spoke, I looked over Lina's shoulder at Richard who raised his glass to me and silently watched us and I realised that I had not seen him for a few days and that I had missed him.

Redcliffe Manor seemed to have cast a spell over me and I realised I had not been the same since entering its doors. I smiled at my employer just as the gloves reached my elbow and I realised that Verity had intercepted our glances, mine and Richard's.

* * *

I was surprised that evening to see Jonathon and Georgina at the dining table. Jonathon was quiet as he acknowledged me whereas Georgina in her overbearing manner greeted me with gusto.

'Darling, how lovely to see you. I was at the dressmakers when you called by today. My dress is ready for the coming out ball.'

Georgina's words surprised me as I had not thought she was attending the ball this week, but I kept my surprise a secret and showed an interest I did not feel.

'May I ask what you are to wear?' I enquired kindly.

'You may indeed, Charlotte,' proceeded Jonathon's sister. 'I am to wear a green gown of silk with flounces of lace on the bodice and skirt and of all things a tiara.'

'You will look delightful, I am sure,' Richard's words surprised me for normally he would not enlist himself in Georgina's conversations. In fact, all at the table looked at him with disbelief and he proceeded, 'But none will match my daughter Lina's beauty on Friday.'

'Thank you, Papa,' Lina said proudly.

'I agree with your father, Lina,' added Verity who rarely spoke unless spoken to. A silence ensued for a couple of minutes when Richard suddenly spoke out of the blue. 'Charlotte had a stroke of good fortune last week,' he said, raising his glass of red wine to his lips. My cheeks grew hot at his words and although I had said it wasn't a secret, I wished heartily that Richard hadn't mentioned my inheritance at the dining table.

'Come, tell us your news,' Georgina said loudly as all eyes watched.

'Just very recently, I have had the good fortune to gain a small inheritance,' I said meekly, looking at Jonathon for some kind of support.

'It's hardly small, Charlotte, come on now, tell them all, my dear.'

Richard's words were like a dagger through my heart.

'Say nothing if you don't wish to,' Jonathon uttered quietly and I looked at him gratefully.

'That is true, my dear, keep quiet for it is no one's business but yours' agreed Verity.

'For goodness sake tell us, Charlotte,' laughed Georgina, 'or none of us will sleep in our beds this night.'

'Have you inherited some trinket that

will pay for your gown?' Georgina's words enraged me and I wished to wipe the smile off her face. I disliked her so much before, but now I loathed her.

I got to my feet. 'If you must know, I have inherited a gold watch.'

'What did I tell you?' sneered Georgina interrupting me

' . . . and,' I emphasised the word, 'and the sum of five thousand pounds.'

There was suddenly a deathly silence but Richard broke it. Richard, who I'd admired all these months from afar.

'So, she's a good catch, eh, Jonathon?' he said looking at Georgina's brother. 'Well, let the best man win.'

After these words, Richard staggered to his feet as he raised a toast to me and I realised with some disdain and disappointment that my employer was intoxicated with liquor.

That night, lying in my bed in the dark, tears trickling down my cheeks, I thought of this eventful day's happenings; meeting Miss Curtis, and her words when she left which were not such a mystery now, for things in this household weren't as I thought.

Redcliffe Manor came to mind and the forgotten rooms, also Jonathon's words, 'I shall live for our next meeting', and above all, Richard Roseby's drunken words at the dining table when I'd wished the ground had swallowed me up and I prayed this wasn't the state of things to come and suddenly realised that Verity Hawksworth had said absolutely nothing which led me to believe that she already knew of my good fortune and only one person could have told her.

7

The following morning, after that disastrous evening, I drew back the curtains and to my delight I could see sunshine instead of rain. I washed and dressed in my most becoming pale blue day dress with a high neckline that was adorned by a pretty cream lace collar, just in case I encountered Richard Roseby. Feeling well dressed would give me the confidence to face him and show him how displeased I was with him even though he was my employer. As things were to turn out, I need not have worried.

Lina and I were making our way down to breakfast and on the first landing we met Lina's father.

'Good morning, daughter,' he greeted Lina, planting a kiss on her cheek, 'and good morning to you, Miss Trent,' he uttered quietly, hardly able to look me in the eye. 'Would you kindly come to my study for a moment, for there is something I wish to say to you?'

'I don't know that I have time, Mr Roseby,' I replied, for the last thing I wanted was to be alone with him when only yesterday morning it would have been everything I wanted.

'Please, Miss Trent, I will only keep you for a moment or two,' he seemed to be pleading with me.

'Will you be all right, Lina, to go on down to breakfast without me?' I asked my charge who was silently watching the scene between her father and I and I set to wondering what she had made of last night's charade.

'It is all right, Charlotte,' Lina agreed in a very grown up fashion. 'You take as long as you like, I'll go on ahead of you.'

'Don't forget Mrs Rivers is due at ten,' I reminded her, as she started walking down the stairs. I followed Richard into his study and sat down on the chair he indicated which reminded

110

me of how all this began. Richard, however, did not sit down. He paced backwards and forwards from my chair to the window, his hands clenched behind his back. He eventually stopped his pacing and stood before me.

'I would like to apologise profusely for my behaviour at the dinner table last night,' he began, 'and I trust, Miss Trent, that you can forgive me.'

So, I thought, we are back on formal terms and I really didn't know if I could forgive him. I looked him up and down which must have distracted him for he went over to the window once more.

'Lina is continuing her dancing lessons today.' At his words, I realised that the apology was forgotten and obviously of little consequence, for I had not even spoken of it nor had the chance and guessed my employer assumed that I was ready to forgive his behaviour of the previous evening so I chose to ignore it as well, saying, 'If this is the case, could I please have the rest of the day off after Mrs Rivers has gone as I have a desire to purchase a couple of items in town, Mr Roseby and I may not get another chance before the ball?' I spoke with a tremble in my voice for I could not believe that the rapport my employer and I had built up over the past few months had trickled away overnight.

'Do you dance, Miss Trent?' His question took me by surprise.

'Yes, I do' I answered quietly, 'although not expertly, but I can get by.'

'Splendid,' Richard replied coming back to his desk and seating himself on the chair behind it. 'You may take the afternoon off, Miss Trent and I trust you will find the articles you need in town.' At which words he perused a letter in front of him and I guessed the meeting was over.

Still feeling somewhat peeved at the way things had gone with my employer earlier, I greeted Mrs Rivers and her two seamstresses who arrived promptly at ten o'clock. As they laid the completed gowns on Lina's bed, she practically jumped up and down with excitement, but I did not reprimand her on this occasion, as I felt an anticipation myself at seeing my completed gown. I wasn't to be disappointed at the finished result as I tried it on the blue skirt swirling around my ankles as I turned to look in the mirror.

'I am more than delighted at the finished result,' I told Mrs Rivers honestly. I glanced across to see Lina twirling around in her ball gown and I smiled for she looked every inch the young lady in a pink silk gown of sophisticated lines with little to adorn it other than deep pink flowers at the hem line, waist and shoulder.

'You look charming, Lina,' I enthused, my own dress forgotten as I walked across to stand before my charge, feeling quite elated at the change in her since I had arrived at Middlepark. Lina's eyes sparkled and she clapped her hands together.

'Oh, Charlotte,' she whispered, 'I can

hardly believe it is me and I can't wait to show father.'

'Your father will be very proud of you,' I told her, my words reminding me of last evening's conversation at the dining table, which caused a cloud to hover over my delight.

'If you are happy with your gowns, Miss Trent, could we please be excused as I have another establishment to visit this morning before lunch?' Mrs Rivers' words cut across our revelry.

'Why of course, Mrs Rivers, we must not delay you but, before you go, there is something I would like to ask you.' As I spoke, I turned away from Lina and steered Mrs Rivers towards the dressing table, where on my arrival I had placed my sketch pad. I could see Lina and one of Mrs Rivers' assistants divesting Lina of her beautiful gown, so I picked up my sketch pad and continued, 'I know there are only a few days, but will it be possible please, to make me a gown for the ball?'

'I don't know if that will be possible

in the time allotted to me,' the dressmaker began.

'I will pay you well, Mrs Rivers, it is a simple style,' and so saying, I showed her the sketch I had drawn.

'Well, I could do my best, Miss Trent, but you will need to try it on and collect the gown from my premises in town for I shall not have the time to come here again,' she said begrudgingly.

'Thank you so much. If it is not ready, I will understand for I realise you are very busy.' My words I knew were true for I had been told that this lady was very much in demand by the gentry here about.

'What colour would you like the gown to be stitched in, Miss, bearing in mind you will have to rely on my judgement.' As she spoke Mrs Rivers took the sketch from me.

'A pale green silk with a cream inset please, Mrs Rivers, and may I say that I trust you completely,' I assured her.

'Very well, Miss Trent, I shall do my

best. If you could call by Thursday afternoon, that would suit me and hopefully give me time. It is fortunate I have your measurements. If there is nothing else, I really must be on my way.' As she spoke, Mrs Rivers beckoned to her girls and as they made their way from Lina's room, the dressmaker turned to me and said, 'Your sketch is very informative. You have a rare talent for drawing.' With which words she closed the door behind her.

Lina ran across to me and hugged me.

'I can hardly wait for the ball, Charlotte,' she said with enthusiasm, twirling me around the room in the steps of a waltz.

'I can understand your impatience, Lina,' I said laughing breathlessly, as I brought her to a halt, and led her by the hand over to the wardrobe to admire the beautiful pink ball gown. The silk shimmered in the light and small pearls sewn painstakingly to the bodice and edges of the short puffed sleeves, set the gown off perfectly. Small dark pink roses looking as if they had just been picked from the garden, adorned the full hemline, one side of the tiny waistline and one shoulder. Gently, I ran my hands across the material and marvelled at its perfection.

'You will be the belle of the ball,' I said gently to Lina, 'and imagine the long white silk gloves and your pretty white slippers. You will captivate all the young men there.'

'You will too, dear Charlotte. I guess Mrs Rivers is to make you a gown too?' Lina queried quietly.

'You are correct in that assumption, but please tell no one, not that it's a secret,' I assured her, 'more a surprise.'

'I shall speak of it to no one, all I ask is that I can accompany you on Thursday.' As she spoke, Lina giggled quietly and took my hand. So the minx had overheard my conversation with Mrs Rivers, but what did it matter.

'There is no other person I would wish to see my new gown with than you' I assured her.

'Then so be it' Lina said with a sigh and I once again realised that this lovely girl had become a young woman over night.

I set off for the town of Budleigh Salterton just after one thirty that afternoon. I wore my light brown serge suit to keep me warm, the skirts around my ankles warm as I walked, my beige bonnet decorated with red flowers bobbing up and down, as I went on my way, enjoying the freedom and fresh air and thinking of recent events. I didn't know how I felt about my employer, Richard Roseby, after yesterday evening's scene at the dining table. He had certainly gone down in my estimation and yet I still felt a warm glow when I thought of him as now and realised that his rudeness yesterday could be an isolated incident.

I stepped onto the path which led along by the sea, stopping for a few minutes to breathe in the salty air. The sun still shone, casting a pale golden light across the water. Lobster pots lay in the sunshine across parts of the pebbled beach and young boys sat on pieces of wood listening to an old mariner's stories of the sea.

I walked on along the path watching the waves gently lapping the shoreline, causing the large grey pebbles to glint in the sunlight as the water splashed upon them. I observed the large hotel on my right, the beautifully landscaped lawns stretching nearly down to the road with pink walls bathed in watery sunlight.

Stepping across the small white wooden bridge that spanned a gurgling brook beneath, I marvelled at the beauty of it all and wished in that moment in time to never leave either Middlepark or this area but I knew that Lina would not need me much longer, except maybe for friendship and I knew in my heart I was daydreaming again having no notion then, what the not too distant future had in store for me.

As I left the seashore behind me and

stepped into the small town, its main street dominated on one side by the brook that ran on its merry way, with small paths spanning it here and there leading to various establishments. I passed a Silversmiths, its gleaming window displaying it's sparkling wares of watches and tankards. The next shop was a large Drapers that took up at least three premises and next door to it was the Millinery and Clothing shop where I had been heading for.

As I pressed down the brass handle and stepped through the door, a bell jangled shrilly through the large interior. It appeared I was the only customer. The shop held a certain pleasant aroma of bee's wax and I could see why as I saw the gleaming wooden counter behind which stood a short middle aged woman in a dove grey dress, the bodice buttoned to the high neckline, which was adorned with a black collar. 'Can I help you, Miss?' the assistant uttered, her blue eyes appraising me as she spoke, her grey hair pulled back into a knot at the back of her head, tendrils of white escaping each side of her plump cheery face.

'Indeed, I hope you can,' I replied, casting my eyes around the goods for sale, when my eyes came to rest on what I was seeking, so I continued, 'Fans for a ball are what I would like to purchase, please, and I see you have a splendid assortment on the shelf.'

'We have all colours, Miss, if you would like to take a closer look.' As she spoke, the assistant moved over to a shelf further along behind the counter and I followed.

'What colour have you in mind, Miss?' I was asked and being shown a beautiful pale blue fan decorated with tiny blue flowers.

'It is lovely,' I enthused, 'but not a suitable colour. I have my eye on the pink one which will suit a young lady and her gown admirably.' As I spoke, I was handed the said fan. It was very delicate, made of pink silk and decorated at the edges with light beige intricately stitched lace and I could imagine Lina fanning herself with it at the ball, while peeping over the top of it secretly, at a suitable young man.

'Can I show you another, Miss?' This time the woman's voice held a querying tone.

'Miss Trent,' I accommodated her. 'I shall purchase this one, please, but I would like to see another.' As I spoke, I cast my eye over the remaining selection of fans. My eyes caught a cream coloured one, totally made of fine lace and on indicating it, the assistant handed it to me. I placed the pink one for Lina on the counter and held the cream lace one offered to me in my gloved hand. It was exquisite in its simplicity and I had never owned such a beautiful object before.

My mind was made up and on telling the woman this, she took two long boxes from under the counter, expertly placing both fans in them and deftly wrapping them in brown paper tied with string. While she did this I looked through the glass front of the counter at what the deep wooden drawers held on display. There were pantaloons, chemises and nightgowns and then my eyes rested on a drawer full of lovely handkerchiefs in pretty pastel colours edged with lace.

'Is there something else I can help you with, Miss Trent?' the woman asked in a respectful tone, something else I was unaccustomed to.

'Yes, please. I will take two of those pretty pink hankies and I think that will be all, thank you,' I said in a satisfied manner, for I was sure Lina would be delighted with my gifts to her and I was very happy with my own purchase.

Having paid the woman with coins from my reticule, I left the shop with my two small parcels and bumped headlong into a gentleman. My parcels scattered themselves across the road and as I bent to pick them up at the same time as the young man, our eyes met and I realised with some pleasure it was Jonathon.

'Miss Trent,' he said. 'I am so sorry,' he apologised, gathering up my parcels in his strong hands and handing them to me.

'It is nothing I assure you, in fact it was my fault for not looking where I was going,' and I smiled at him wishing to break into laughter but he looked so contrite.

'Please say you will come with me to the Tea Rooms across the street and take a cup of afternoon tea with me and maybe a pastry,' he implored earnestly. How could I resist such a request?

'I would be happy to,' I agreed taking his arm as he led me across the street and we stepped over the tiny bridge that spanned the brook to the Tea Rooms.

Inside the establishment was quite small with tables for three scattered around covered with pristine white tablecloths. About half a dozen people were enjoying their fare and for a ghostly second or two it went very quiet as we walked in and seated ourselves by the window, Jonathon pulling the black varnished chair out for me, the conversation resumed. Almost immediately, a waitress placed a cake stand on the table which boasted various small cakes decorated in icing sugar and coloured marzipan.

'Would you like to order tea, Sir?' the woman asked. I was fascinated by her white lacey mop cap covering her curly ginger coloured hair, matched by a starched white apron that reached nearly to the bottom of her black dress.

'Would you care for tea?' Jonathon asked me.

'That would be very enjoyable, thank you,' I said looking at him and then at the young woman who had taken our order. While we waited for our tea to be brought, Jonathon and I engaged in a pleasant conversation about the forthcoming ball.

'Are you looking forward to it?' my companion asked of me.

'I am indeed, Sir. It will be a new experience for me,' I told him, 'for I have never attended such an occasion before.'

'Dare I ask that you would do me the honour of dancing with me?'

Jonathon was very serious as he spoke, his lovely eyes looking deeply into mine and for a second I was spellbound by his good looks, his gentle voice — and his question.

'Yes, Mr Moore,' I said finding my voice, 'I will dance with you.'

'Your promise is sweet to my ears, Miss Trent, and I thank you for it. May the moment arrive quicker than I could hope for,' my companion told me earnestly, just as the waitress arrived at our table with a large tray laden with cups, saucers, plates, milk jug, sugar basin and a large tea pot, all matching in beautifully decorated porcelain of green with tiny pink rosebuds.

I removed my gloves and poured the tea for both of us, thinking of Jonathon's request for a dance and the sweet words he had spoken.

'Would you care for a cake?' This

lovely young man's words cut across my thoughts of him and I picked a tiny square sponge cake decorated with pink fondant. As I bit delicately into it, I noticed Jonathon was looking into his cup of amber liquid, twiddling the teaspoon in his saucer and as I watched him he suddenly looked at me and said quietly, 'It is a delicate subject, Miss Trent, but I wish to know if Richard Roseby has apologised for his ungallant behaviour of yesterday evening.' He spoke more passionately than normal and I could see anger in his eyes.

'He has, indeed,' I began laying the remains of my cake on the tiny plate in front of me 'but whether I could accept that apology is another matter.'

'You must know I did not condone the man's behaviour, Miss Trent and I certainly would not look upon you as a challenge or a prize to be bandied around between two men.' As he spoke the words, Jonathon covered my hand gently with his and took it away just as quickly.

'I am sorry, Miss Trent, but I am angry.'

'Then please be angry no longer and know that I believe what you say,' I murmured. 'Now please join me in partaking of one of these delicious little cakes.' We both laughed and the serious moment was gone and we sat sipping our tea in happy companionship.

As the bell jingled, we both looked up and to my amazement it was Miss Curtis, Lina's nurse, who had stepped into the Tea Room and she came across to us.

'How nice to see you, Miss Trent and you, Mr Moore. It is getting chilly outside and I thought to warm myself with a hot drink,' said Miss Curtis with great gusto.

'Please join us, Miss Curtis, if that pleases Miss Trent.' As Jonathon spoke, he looked enquiringly at me.

'Yes, please do,' I agreed. 'Far better to sit with us than on your own.' So it was that Lina's nurse pulled up a chair and joined us for afternoon tea, the three of us chatting quietly and I arrived at the conclusion that Miss Curtis was in fact a very pleasant woman.

Some time later, as the three of us stepped outside onto the street, Jonathon turned to pass the time of day with a gentleman who was passing by and Miss Curtis took hold of my arm gently and said quietly, 'I need to speak with you alone, Miss Trent.' As she spoke, she glanced at Jonathon and continued. 'It is important, but please tell no one.'

'Very well, Miss Curtis, for you have intrigued me, but where and when?' I asked of her very quickly for Jonathon was already saying his farewell to his gentleman friend.

'I live at Holly Cottage. Anyone will tell you where it is,' the nurse said just as Jonathon turned back to us.

'Well ladies, can I escort you home?' he asked of us, smiling.

'As for me, I have a couple of things to purchase, but thank you for your kind offer,' said Miss Curtis and turning to me she said 'I hope to see you before too long, Miss Trent. Now I'll bid you both good day and thank you for the tea and enjoyable company.' With those words, she headed off across the street leaving me quite perplexed.

I took the arm Jonathon offered and accepted his company for the walk home, my brown paper parcels clutched in my hand. The watery sun was dropping in the sky and left little reflection now on the sea, which looked murky and grey. The children were gone as was the mariner they had been talking to but lobster pots were still strewn here and there, waiting no doubt for tomorrow's fishing trip.

'You've never told me anything of your life, Miss Trent,' Jonathon said so suddenly it made me jump.

'There is little to tell, except I was born in Topsham and both of my parents are dead,' I said rather woefully.

'I am sorry to hear about your parents, ours died long ago too.

Georgina has looked after me for as long as I can remember, although I do have memories of my mother at Redcliffe, but let us not dwell on the past, it is the future which is important, and Miss Trent.'

Here, Jonathon stopped walking and turned me towards him. 'Lovely Miss Trent, I confess I would like you to be part of my future.' At his words I turned away from him and he misconstrued my action. 'I apologise, Miss Trent, I have upset you, I shouldn't have spoken,' he apologised.

'No, no, you misunderstand, Mr Moore, I am flattered by your words, but at this moment in time, have no ready answer for them.'

'Please do not be apologetic. Come now, let us walk on and I will think of what you have said,' I assured him and I took his arm once more, smiling at him and he smiled in return which warmed my heart. Little more was said as we walked until we reached the gates of Middlepark.

'I shall not see you now until the ball no doubt' Jonathon said turning me towards him. 'It was fortuitous that I bumped into you in town, for I have enjoyed our afternoon together.'

'I have enjoyed it as much,' I told him honestly for I had but I was unsure of my feelings for him or my employer. As I looked across to the door of Middlepark, I could see that the door was open and Richard Roseby stood on the step watching us.

'I shall have to go, Jonathon. Thank you for your company today and I will look forward to seeing you at the ball,' I said not wishing Jonathon to see my employer standing there.

Thankfully, he did not. He raised my hand to his lips and looking into my eyes Jonathon said, 'Farewell pretty maiden and please do not forget your promise to me.' With which words he walked away, not looking back for which I was thankful. As I walked up the path, Richard had disappeared through the front door leaving it ajar for me, but as I stepped into the small hallway he was waiting for me. My heart skipped a beat for I was sure that in some way he was going to admonish me but he said curtly, 'I shall be away for a couple of days, Miss Trent. I have hired a large carriage to take us to Kilkenny Hall. I will be grateful if you and Lina could be ready and waiting at six o'clock, please. I bid you goodnight, Miss Trent.'

So saying he made his way to the drawing room without waiting for an answer. To say I was a trifle upset by this interlude was an understatement. As I made my way up to my room I could feel hot tears stinging at my eyes, but as I entered my room it was forgotten, because across my mirror, scrawled in red rouge, was the word ANNA. I was as perplexed at this as much as Miss Curtis' words earlier and I lay awake for some time in bed that night mulling it all over in my mind, Miss Curtis, Anna, Jonathon, Richard Roseby and Madeline and I really didn't know who or what mattered most.

8

Thursday arrived. I had been awoken in the early hours by a thunderstorm and by seven o'clock was washed and dressed in my new blue gown, ready with anticipation for our visit to Mrs Rivers' establishment in the town. Richard Roseby, my employer, was indeed absent from Middlepark and I had not seen any sight of Verity Hawksworth either and had set to wondering if they were at some place unknown together. I was also still mulling over the name which had been etched on my dressing table mirror two evenings ago.

While I was waiting for Lina to go down to breakfast with her, I went to my drawer and uncovered the small bundle of letters that had been written to Madeline. Taking them from the drawer and looking down at the red ribbon, which bound them together, I walked over to the window and drawing back the curtains looked down at the oak tree. Its branches were still laden with leaves which were slowly starting to change colour.

Raindrops glistened on the branches and, although it had been raining earlier on, I could see that hopefully, we were to enjoy some pleasant weather today, for which I was thankful.

Looking back at the letters clutched in my hand, I thought of the words *Trust no one but Anna*. But who was Anna? Did she still live or had she died long ago taking Madeline's secret with her to the grave? And what of Madeline and the child? These were questions that may never be answered but someone within these walls was keeping the story alive but who? My employer? Lina? But no, she was far too young to know of this story of Madeline. And what of the sister, Joanna, who was mentioned? At this thought, I felt quite elated for it would be a start if I could find out about Joanna. Maybe there was a family Bible. After the ball this would be my quest, to find out more about the Roseby family. I also knew that I must hand the letters over to Richard, my employer, for after all, it was his home and his mystery, but it was also my mystery now and I intended to pursue it. With this thought in mind, I placed the bundle of missives back in the drawer and vowed to hand them over to my employer the day after the ball.

'Charlotte!' Lina greeted me with excitement in her voice. 'It is today we go to see your gown.'

'It is indeed, Lina and I am as full of expectancy as you, but I have encountered a problem,' I told her.

'What problem could there possibly be?' asked Lina solemnly.

'With your father not here,' I began, 'we will have no way of bringing the gown back with us, that is of course, if Mrs Rivers has had time to make it.'

'I am sure that knowing the circumstances, Mrs Rivers will deliver the gown,' said Lina, quite sure of herself. 'And if there is no gown, what will you wear, Charlotte?' This question was one I had been asking myself while the thunder rumbled earlier.

'That I will decide on after we have visited Mrs Rivers,' I told her, with more conviction that I actually felt.

Over breakfast, Lina and I talked of the coming ball for it was uppermost in both our minds. 'I am told by my dancing tutor that we are to curtsey as our partner bows before each dance,' said Lina, nibbling at her bread and butter. 'Did you know this, Charlotte?'

'Yes, I had read about it, but never actually curtseyed,' I answered.

'Then we shall practice this morning after breakfast, for I have mastered it to perfection, or so Mrs Knowles, my dance instructor told me only yesterday afternoon.' As she was speaking, I looked at Lina. She wore one of her new day gowns of a pale blue heavy cotton, the long sleeves tapering to her wrists edged with white lace as was the v-neckline and no other adornment whatsoever and yet she looked beautiful in a gentle way and with her lovely blond hair shining in the daylight, which filtered through the large dining room window, She also looked very serene.

'Yes, of course, Lina. I would dearly love some tuition in the niceties of dancing,' I told her as I sipped my coffee.

'It will be great fun,' Lina continued. 'And did you know that all the gentlemen will wear white gloves so as to not cause their sweaty palms to touch ours and a gentleman can only ask us to bestow on him one dance.'

'Oh I am so looking forward it.' Lina sighed, a far-away look on her face.

After breakfast we made our way to my room. 'I have something for you, Lina, a present from me to mark your coming out ball' I told her as we entered the room.

'I adore surprises. Whatever it is, I know I shall love it.' Lina clapped her hands as she spoke while I went to a drawer and retrieved the box which held the fan. I passed it to her and she took the long box from me and sat upon my bed to open it. As she removed the lid, and peeled back the tissue paper, a cry of delight escaped her lips as she looked at me.

'My dear Charlotte, a fan — and a truly lovely one to match my gown. Oh thank you so much, but . . . ' And here she faltered. 'I have no knowledge of how to use one. What shall I do?'

'We will learn together for I have bought myself one and have little idea either.' At my words, we both laughed and sped to Lina's room to practise with the fans and curtseying.

We both got the idea of using the fans very easily. It was a question of opening them and closing them with one hand, which we practiced over and over. It required a certain flourish of the wrist and eventually, we both mastered the art at the same time and then Lina went across to the large wardrobe to look at her gown and squealed with delight as the colour matched her gown perfectly, for which I was thankful.

'Now,' said Lina, 'I have to give you some instruction in the art of the curtsey.' Lina's curtsey flowed with her, but it was harder to accomplish than I had anticipated and on more than one occasion nearly fell over amongst shrieks of laughter. But, by the time luncheon was ready, my curtsey was passable and we went down to lunch in a very happy companionable frame of mind.

Suddenly, I realised that Lina would not need me much longer and would no doubt be a married woman within the year. This realisation troubled me for what would I do when I left Middlepark, but as it happened, my future was already planned out and it was only I who knew nothing about it yet.

I did not let this thought trouble me as Lina and I set off for the town and Mrs Rivers' dressmaking establishment.

We walked in silence, side by side, until we stepped onto the path which ran alongside the sea.

'Lina, I hope you don't mind me asking,' I ventured, 'but is there a family Bible belonging to the Roseby family?' I had been wanting to ask this all day and had at last, plucked up the courage, hoping that Lina would not think my question strange and ask me why I had asked it but I need not have worried.

'Yes, there is one, it is quite large and very heavy, so it is kept in the large church in the next village of East Budleigh,' she told me and thankfully, her voice held no suspicion.

'Has Miss Hawksworth gone away as well, Lina?' I asked her, 'I haven't seen her since your father left on Tuesday.'

'Yes, she has gone to stay with a friend who lives near Exeter as she needed to collect her new gown,' Lina told me quite readily, 'and I think father said she would meet us at Kilkenny Hall and then come home with us. Did you know, Charlotte, that the ball doesn't start until nine at night and does not end until the early hours of the morning?'

'If this is the case,' I told her, 'we must rest all day tomorrow.' She heartily agreed, and shortly after we arrived at the dressmakers.

The premises was a small house at the other end of the main street with a door to one side of a large window that gleamed, the net curtains white as snow. This was only to be expected of Mrs Rivers, I thought as we waited for an answer to our knock. We were ushered by a young maid with shiny black hair beneath her white mop cap, into the front parlour, which was quite small and seeming even smaller due to the small tables against two walls holding an abundance of various trinkets.

A large picture of a stern looking man hung over the black leaded grate, which looked bleak and forlorn and I guessed that once a fire was lit in its depth the whole room would look far more warm and cosy than now for it was very dismal. Lina and I sat on high backed chairs awaiting Mrs Rivers. When she walked into the room, Mrs Rivers looked as always, calm and collected and stern like the man in the picture, I thought.

'Your gown is ready, Miss Trent, if you would like to follow me, please.' As she spoke, Lina and I rose from our seats and followed Mrs Rivers through the door and along a long dark hallway to the back of the house, where we stepped into a light airy room so much in contrast to the parlour we had left, I almost gasped with surprise. There was a curtained area on one side of the spacious room and before me, on a tailor's dummy, was my gown. Tears sprung to my eyes, for I had expected a lovely gown, but not one so perfect and beautiful as the one I looked at now. Mrs Rivers had followed the sketch I had drawn with accuracy, but it was the material she had used to make this creation which took my breath away.

The close fitting off the shoulder bodice and full skirt had been fashioned in a cream silk georgette with pale green flowers embroidered at the neckline, which matched perfectly the yards of pale green muslin that fell apart at the front to reveal the cream silk skirt. I went over to look at it more closely.

'You are pleased, Miss Trent?' Mrs Rivers asked.

'I am more than pleased, Mrs Rivers,' I said looking in her direction. 'It is a work as such that I had not imagined.'

'Try it on please, Charlotte,' Lina urged and until I heard her voice, I realised I had quite forgotten she was there.

'Yes, Miss Trent, please let us fit it for I need to know if the hemline is the correct length,' said Mrs Rivers in her controlled voice, so I was helped out of my blue gown by one of Mrs Rivers' seamstresses, who I gathered was called Daisy and an excited Lina. I stepped into the dress as small cream silk buttons with loops to secure them fastened all the way down the back, which took Daisy and Lina several minutes to secure. It was a perfect fit except for the length by a couple of inches. My heart sank.

'Do not be alarmed, Miss Trent, for my girls will adjust the length and I can bring it to you tomorrow afternoon,' said Mrs Rivers kindly and I breathed a sigh of relief while I looked down on the skirts of cream and pale green, marvelling at my good fortune.

'You look beautiful, Charlotte,' Lina said honestly. 'The colour green becomes you. This has made me long even more for tomorrow, for we will both look like princesses, you and I.' I believed that her words were true and longed for tomorrow myself, but the question burned in my mind, did I wish to look captivating for Richard Roseby or Jonathon Moore?

Dressed back in the clothes that I had arrived in and ready to leave, thanking Mrs Rivers from the bottom of my heart, the dressmaker took hold of my arm gently and took me back into the dressing room.

'Miss Trent,' she began quietly, 'I have a proposition for you.'

'And what would that be, Mrs Rivers for I am certainly not a seamstress,' I told her, quite bemused by her words,

'No, Miss Trent. It has nothing to do with stitching, but drawing,' she enlightened me.

'In what way?' I asked of her, quite perplexed now.

'Your sketch, Miss Trent of this beautiful gown I have made you was quite outstanding and I was hoping you may like to sketch styles for me, as fashion decrees, of course, for which I will pay you,' Mrs Rivers told me.

'You wish to employ me is what you are saying?' I asked, quite taken aback at this turn of events.

'That is exactly what I am proposing, Miss Trent, yes,' Mrs Rivers ascertained and I was quite dumbfounded for a moment and unable to answer her. It was true I thought that I loved sketching, but would I wish to do it for a living was the question, and what of Middlepark and Lina.

'Please let me think about it for a few days,' I said, 'for this has come as a shock as you can imagine and there is a lot to take into account.'

'I quite understand, Miss Trent, and shall look forward to hearing your decision, in shall we say, a couple of weeks?' Mrs Rivers suggested.

'Why, yes, thank you. That is a reasonable amount of time to think something over. I look forward to receiving my gown tomorrow, thank you,' with which words, I turned to join Lina, my mind in turmoil.

★   ★   ★

The day of the ball had finally arrived. After breakfast, Lina and I rested in our rooms, even though Lina was feverish with excitement, which after luncheon could not be contained.

'Oh, Charlotte!' she said bursting

into my room while I was resting on my bed, thoughts of recent events whirling in my mind and wondering when I would find the chance to visit Miss Curtis. Everything was intriguing from Madeline to Miss Curtis' words. I arose from the bed, rest over for the day.

'What time will we need to get ready, Charlotte and shall we get everything together that we need, gloves, slippers, reticule and our gowns,' shrieked Lina all in one sentence that I was glad when four o'clock arrived and we were to start getting ready. Mrs Rivers had delivered my gown an hour before and all was well now. Ruby and I helped Lina into her gown and slippers and while Ruby fashioned Lina's hair, I went to my room to get myself attired for the all important ball. My hands trembled as I stepped into my beautiful gown, knowing that I would need help to do the buttons up, I went bare footed along to Lina's room when I was startled by my employer.

'You are captivating, Miss Trent,' he

said and I whirled around to see Richard standing there looking at me, a secret smile on his face. I was very much aware that my dress was undone at the back and my hair in disarray.

'Mr Roseby,' I stammered. 'I had not thought to see you on this landing.'

'That much is obvious, Charlotte,' he said walking towards me, the smile still on his face which unnerved me somewhat.

'May I do the buttons up for you,' he continued, stepping closer.

'Indeed not, Sir,' I said angrily and hastened away to Lina's room.

At quarter to six we were both ready. Ruby had done wonders with our hair. I stepped back from Lina and was astounded at the total transformation in her now that her hair was swept up on the top of her head, a pink feather adorning it. She looked every inch the young lady and her gown was exquisite as she indeed looked herself.

'You look wonderful, Lina,' I told her, a tremor in my voice. 'Your father will be so proud of you.' As I spoke the words, I thought of Richard as I was still smarting from his impudent behaviour earlier.

'Now let me look at you,' said Lina. 'In fact, let us look in the mirror side by side.' The reflection that we saw was almost unreal, for I didn't look like me at all. Never before had I worn, or indeed owned, such a lovely gown. My hair was swept back with small curls dancing each side of my face and the curly fringe resting perfectly on my forehead.

I had purchased the cream silk slippers on my way back from my outing with Lina and I could see them now peeping out from below the lovely skirt of my gown. Our long white gloves, which we had more trouble with getting on than anything, set our gowns off perfectly, our skin gleaming in the light. Lina and I both had to walk carefully down the two flights of stairs, gathering our gowns at the front, lest we fall.

On reaching the small hallway, Lina's father took one look at his daughter and the love and pride on his face was evident. 'You look adorable child and I fear that I may lose you tonight to some fortunate young suitor.' As he spoke, Richard walked towards her and gently kissed her cheek. He looked very handsome himself in black with a white starched shirt and white bow at his neck and indeed as Lina had told me, white gloves.

The large carriage was waiting for us and we settled ourselves in it for the journey to Kilkenny Hall. I drifted into a half slumber, my thoughts of the man who sat opposite me, his eyes appraising me, his daughter at his side, her arm linked through his and I knew that whatever else I thought of Richard Roseby, there was no doubt he adored his lovely daughter.

On arriving at Kilkenny Hall, which boasted a very long driveway, it was dark and light spilled from the large doorway and the downstairs windows. I felt very nervous as Richard helped me from the carriage and Lina and I smoothed our skirts ready for our entrance to this magnificent building. The ballroom was vast with garlands of green festooning the walls. Three large chandeliers hung from the ceiling lit by hundreds of candles, their glow casting a mellow light over the many ladies and gentlemen who moved around the room, the ladies causing a riot of colour. In a large alcove, tables were laden with food.

I was mesmerised by the whole scene and especially the large orchestra congregated at the far end of the hall. Lina's father seated us on red velvet seats and went to get us some refreshment of cool lemonade for the hall was hot. As I watched, Lina flicked her fan open, fanning herself with it while watching the scene before her. Verity arrived looking as lovely and serene as ever in a beige silk gown adorned here and there with silver sequins sparkling in the light of the candles as she walked gracefully towards us. I was sipping the lemonade when the orchestra struck up to the strains of the Strauss Waltz.

Gentlemen were bowing before ladies and leading them to the floor and they did indeed bow and curtsey and within seconds there was a young man of pleasing appearance with blond hair bowing before Lina who gracefully accepted his polite request for a dance. I watched them as they glided around the floor wondering what they were speaking of when Richard stood before me and my heart lurched, whether it was with pleasure or dismay I honestly could not say. Richard bowed before me.

'May I have the honour of this dance, please, Miss Trent?' he said graciously as I rose from my seat and let him lead me across to the dance floor. Richard gave a slight bow and I a small curtsey as he looked down on me and then his hand was on mine and his other hand resting a little too tightly on my waist.

'I could wait no longer to hold you in my arms, Charlotte,' he whispered as we whirled around the floor, Richard expertly avoiding other dancers. His words in one way surprised me after his curtness the other day and I did not quite feel the pleasure at them as I would have done a week ago. My dancing partner said no more but his hand on my waist was firmer as the dance went on and I was quite relieved when the music stopped and my employer led me back to my seat where I could regain my composure.

Lina was dancing all evening. She must have been exhausted and at one time between dancing she spoke to me, her eyes bright.

'That young man I have just danced with is called Brett and he is heir to the Malverton Estate in North Devon,' she told me. 'He has asked that he may call on me. Isn't it exciting, Charlotte?' as she was whisked away to dance again. I danced intermittently with young gentlemen and more elderly ones. I was beginning to feel tired and while eating a canapé and small sandwiches, I looked up and Jonathon was standing before me. I had never seen him dressed in black before, his fair wavy hair swept back off his face his white gloved hand reaching out to me.

'Will you bestow on me the honour of this next dance, please Miss Trent?' as he bowed slowly before me, his eyes never leaving my face.

'With pleasure, Mr Moore,' I replied, trembling with anticipation I let him lead me to the floor as the orchestra struck up another waltz. Jonathon bowed and I gave a perfect curtsey in return and then his hand held mine while he gently held my waist. As we glided around the floor he never took his eyes off my face and I could feel the soft green muslin of my skirt, flowing as one with me.

'You look enchanting, Miss Trent and at this moment in time, I am the luckiest man in the ballroom,' he whispered and I felt my cheeks go hot, praying he could not see it.

'Thank you, kind sir,' I replied just as the music stopped to my disappointment. Jonathon bowed and led me back to my chair. He walked away and then I saw him glance back at me and our eyes met and for a brief second we were locked together. I sipped at my lemonade and with a flourish of my wrist opened my fan for the first time to cool my hot cheeks.

The evening for Lina was a success as she had a suitor who was to call upon her the next week at Middlepark. As we stood in the entrance hall, awaiting our carriage to pull up at the front of the Hall, I saw Jonathon and Richard standing not far apart from each other. Nonchalantly, I looked from one to the other and I honestly could not say quite where my heart lay, but I was soon to find out.

9

We arrived back at Middlepark at seven o'clock in the morning. Richard bade us goodnight, kissing Lina on the cheek, before we made our way up the stairs. We were both weary, but when we reached her room, Lina fell on to her bed laughing.

'What a wonderful evening,' she said, jumping up once more and taking my hand. 'Please do the honour of dancing with me, Miss Trent,' and as she spoke, she whirled me around her bedroom until I felt dizzy and I felt it was time to calm her down. I stopped her with some resistance, for the young woman was over tired and enraptured by the evening.

'Come now, Lina, we must get you to bed, for sleep is what we both need,' I told her. 'Now be sensible. We have had a wonderful time and can re-live it later in the day when we have rested. Now let us get you ready for bed.' The long gloves were the biggest problem of all, but eventually, both Lina's and mine were strewn across the bed.

'Before I forget,' I asked Lina, 'please undo the buttons on my gown.' She did, far more slowly than they were done up and the task done, she went across and looked at herself in the mirror.

'I don't ever want to take this beautiful gown off,' she said petulantly.

'Well you must, young lady,' I told her firmly and eventually, the gown was hanging on the wardrobe. Her hair was brushed and Lina was in her nightgown. I drew back the covers of her bed and she climbed in, exhausted. I made sure the heavy curtains were pulled to properly so the daylight didn't filter in. Giving Lina a kiss on the cheek, I made to leave when she suddenly said, sleepily, 'I saw you dancing with Father. How I wish that you would marry him,' and then she was asleep and I was left feeling quite confused.

Now, I really didn't know if I would wish to marry my employer, when in the beginning, it was all I dreamt of, but as I undressed, reluctantly stepping out of my gown, I reached the conclusion that I was a daydreamer no longer and as I slipped between the crisp white sheets, promptly fell asleep.

I knew no more until two o'clock that afternoon when I awoke and drew back the curtains to see the afternoon sun shining through my window, casting a strip of light across the carpet. After I was dressed, I remembered that I had vowed to pass Madeline's letters over to my employer.

First, I went to see if Lina was awake and was surprised to see her bed already empty and no sign of her. I set to thinking that I had failed in my duties and should not have slept so long. Swiftly, I returned to my room when I bumped into Ruby, who carried a large tray laden with tea, toast and a boiled egg.

'Master thought you may be in need of refreshment, Miss' Ruby told me 'and when you be ready, he'd like to see you in the drawing-room about three o'clock, but no rush, Miss.' While drinking the well needed cup of tea, I tried to ascertain what my employer wished to see me about and wondered also where Lina was. After the well needed refreshment, I smoothed the skirt of my dove grey dress, checked my hair and retrieved Madeline's letters from my drawer. I looked down at them and the miniature for what would probably be the last time. I felt a pang of sadness, but knew it was the right thing to do.

My hand on the porcelain handle of the drawing room, I hesitated, for I was nervous about handing over the letters, but common sense told me, if I had not chanced upon them, they would still be tucked away beneath the floorboards in my room and would probably never have been found. This thought in mind, I stood up straight, held my head high and entered the room. Richard Roseby was standing with his back to the fireplace, in which a cheery fire burned brightly, taking the chill off the room.

'Charlotte!' my employer exclaimed, using my Christian name once more, 'thank you for joining me. Please be seated.' He indicated the settle to one side of the fire. I placed the letters and miniature beside me but Richard seemed not to notice, he was intent on looking at my face.

'You looked enchanting at the ball, Charlotte,' he began, 'and I realised as I held you and danced with you, that I have fallen in love with you.' His declaration was indeed a shock, for I had certainly not anticipated it. Two weeks ago I would have been elated by it and fallen into his arms, but now I did not know what I felt for this handsome man and realised that for a while now, he had not pervaded my dreams.

'Please speak to me, Charlotte,' he implored.

'I thank you, Mr Roseby, but at this moment in time, I really have no notion as to what to say,' I said honestly and then unexpectedly, Richard was on one knee before me.

'I ask you, Charlotte Trent, to do me the very great honour of becoming my wife,' he said earnestly as he took hold of my hand and looked into my eyes, eyes which must have mirrored the confusion I felt, but an answer was necessary to alleviate its obvious strong emotion.

'I thank you for your proposal, Sir, which to say the least, is unexpected and I ask that I may be given some time to think about it,' I said quietly.

At my words, Richard rose to his feet once more and leaned on the mantelshelf, looking for some time at the flames leaping up the chimney, the only sound being the crackle of the logs and my beating heart.

Then he turned to me. 'I understand that you will need time, Charlotte, but I beg of you that you will give me your answer tomorrow and I pray the answer you give will be, yes,' he told me quite calmly.

'Thank you, Sir, I shall go away to consider your proposal,' I said with far more composure than I felt. I rose from the settle and picked up the precious bundle of letters.

'Before I leave, Sir, I would like to give you these,' I began, handing them to him along with the miniature. As he looked down at them, Richard's face drained of colour, or had I imagined it, but then, I had already agreed with myself that I was no longer a daydreamer.

'Where did you find these, Miss Trent?' he said looking at me. His eyes were cold and I had noted his formal use of addressing me.

'I found them under the floorboards in my room, Sir,' I told him honestly.

'And how the duce did you come to be looking under the floorboards?' he asked angrily.

'Half a crown rolled under my bed

and got lodged between the floorboards in the corner of my room,' I explained, 'and when I dislodged it, the floorboard came with it.'

'Did it indeed? That will be all, Miss Trent. Thank you.' I realised that I was dismissed.

As I stepped back into the hallway, I had reached one conclusion, that my employer, Richard Roseby, was a man of changing moods and I certainly had no intention of marrying him.

I made my way to the kitchen in search of Ruby who may know where Lina had gone. I had never entered this domain before and was surprised to find how small the kitchen was but even so, it boasted a large black cooking range where Ruby sat on a rocking chair, warming her hands by the fire.

'Miss!' Ruby exclaimed, jumping up, causing the chair to rock to and fro on its own.

'I have come to ask if you know where Lina has gone, please, Ruby' I said, half smiling to myself, for Ruby acted like a burglar caught in the act with a silver teapot.

'I think she went out for some fresh air with Miss Verity,' Ruby told me.

'Thank you, Ruby and I am sorry I startled you,' I told her gently.

On my way back across the hall, I decided to go back to the drawing-room to speak to Richard of his proposal, for I had made my mind up and I felt it unfair to keep him waiting for an answer. As I reached the door, I could see that it was ajar and I could hear voices, one was certainly Verity, so I eavesdropped and could hear Verity say, 'So what was her answer?'

Then Richard's voice, 'She said she needed time to think about it, but I can wait no longer.'

So, I thought, as I moved away from the door and made my way up the stairs, my employer cannot wait, well I will keep him dangling a bit longer, I decided, if only to repay him for his bad behaviour at the dining table.

Lina was in her room when I looked

in, propped up by a pillow on her bed. She beckoned for me to sit by her and we spent a pleasant hour talking of the ball and all the young men she had danced with. An hour later, Ruby appeared to say the Master wished to see me in the drawing-room.

'You go on,' said Lina, 'for I could do with a nap, if you could please draw the curtains before you go.' I did as I was bid and made my way once more down the stairs, thinking that Richard could obviously wait no longer, but as I entered the drawing-room he said.

'I wish to take you to meet a friend of mine and if you could please wear your best gown, for it is quite a well-to-do household. Would you care for a small glass of wine?' he asked solicitously.

'I will partake of a glass of wine with you,' I agreed graciously and on being handed a glass of clear liquid, I sat down on the settle and sipped it slowly while we talked of my time here since I had arrived. Richard was charming again and did not once mention

Madeline's letters. The wine finished, I handed my employer the glass and he said, 'I shall be waiting with the pony and trap in half an hour, Charlotte.' And with those words I was once again dismissed.

Hastening back to my room, I wondered who Richard was taking me to see and I prayed he did not intend to introduce me as his betrothed. Back in my room, I decided to wear my new blue silk gown, which should be appropriate for any visit. I tidied my hair and pinched my cheeks applying a little rouge to my lips for I looked quite pale today. Deciding it could be chilly, I wrapped my black cape around my shoulders and placed a blue bonnet on my head. Picking up my reticule, I was ready. Before I went downstairs, I looked in on Lina, quietly opening the door to her room. I could see she was asleep.

Richard was waiting with the pony and trap. He assisted me into it, wrapping a warm blue blanket around my legs, we set off. I'd started to feel strange, my brain didn't seem to be functioning properly and I felt as if I was in a dream but I put it down to tiredness.

'Are you all right, Charlotte? I heard Richard's voice but it seemed to come from a distance.'

'Just tired, Sir,' I managed to utter, my voice not seeming like my own. The sun had gone down and everything seemed very dark. Trees and hedges passed by us and small cottages with plumes of smoke spiralling from the chimneys and I suddenly wished that I was tucked up cosily in a small cottage and safe. Where did that word come from I asked myself and I looked at Richard who appeared to have taken on a look of the Devil himself and suddenly I felt afraid, wondering where my employer was taking me.

'Where are we going, Mr Roseby?' I asked weakly.

I did feel weak, so much so that I leant against him and then had to shake myself upright once more, wondering what could be happening to me.

'Have no fear, Charlotte, we are nearly there.' His voice seemed to come from far away and I was struggling to keep myself awake.

'I feel unwell,' I told the man beside me, my voice shrill as I caught hold of his arm. 'We need to go back, Sir, back to Middlepark,' I pleaded.

'It is probably the evening air, Charlotte, after partaking of the wine,' he assured me and I realised his words could make sense, so I sat as upright as I could, watching as we entered a small village, cottages built in a cluster either side of the winding street.

I noticed that a mist was rising and was sure I was not imagining it. As we drove on, the mist seemed to get deeper, obscuring the cottages and the air was chilled. I shivered and pulled my cape closer around me and then leaned against Richard once more, but this time, I did not have the strength to sit up again. I was half asleep when I felt the pony and trap pull to a halt. Richard moved me away from him and opening my eyes I realised that the mist was now swirling around us, obscuring everything in its path, but I was so pleased we had reached our destination, for I would feel better once we were in a warm room and I was drinking a hot cup of tea.

'I will come round for you, Charlotte.' I heard Richard's voice from far away and didn't care any more where I was or what was happening to me. The next thing I knew I was being lifted from the trap by my employer who steadied me as I struggled to stand.

'Take my arm, Charlotte,' Richard instructed and I did as I was bid, half leaning against him as we walked up a short path, our feet crunching on the gravel. I could not see anything because of the mist, only that a large wooden door lay before us, which Richard was now opening and we passed through into a large dimly lit room with a low ceiling which was very cold and I shivered once more. We seemed to be walking through something on the floor and looking down, I could see it was rose petals strewn across the floor for as far as I could see. My befuddled brain tried to make some sense of it but I could not think straight, as Richard, with me holding on to his arm, came to a halt.

'Where are we?' I asked him quietly, as my brain told me I shouldn't shout, that we were in a place that demanded reverence and then I heard a woman's voice, one I recognised but could not place.

'You took your time, brother.' I heard the words but could not recall where I had heard the voice before and then, through a haze, I saw a tall and thin man standing before us, with grey hair and a long grey beard.

'Who is this, Richard?' I whispered. 'Is it your friend?'

'Yes, my dear, it is. Now listen to what the kind man has to say,' he told me gently. My legs felt weak and I knew, that at any second, they would buckle beneath me and indeed they did. I fell to the ground from Richard's grasp and all I could smell was the heady scent of roses as my head fell on a concrete floor. I closed my eyes, glad to lie down and sleep, but I felt Richard and the woman, whoever she was, pulling me to my feet I smoothed my skirt, brushing the rose petals away and I was once more holding on to Richard's arm, but my mind was beginning to feel less hazy and I was starting to feel more aware of what was happening. I looked at the woman, struggling to recall who she was. She was pretty and dressed well and then it dawned on me.

'Verity,' I almost shouted. 'What are you doing here?'

I strived to free myself from Richard's grasp, realising something was dreadfully amiss, but Richard held on to my arm and spoke to the stranger. 'Please carry on.'

'Are you sure, Sir?' the man asked. 'I

can see the lady is distressed.'

'I am sure and I am paying you well for your services, now please proceed,' Richard ordered.

'Very well, Sir,' the stranger said looking at me with sympathy in his eyes. 'I will begin. Dearly beloved we are gathered together in the sight of God.' At this point, my befuddled mind came to life and I realised with some dismay, that the man was a priest and this was a marriage ceremony with a very reluctant bride.

10

'No!' I shouted, my voice reverberating around what must have been a small chapel.

'Don't fight it, Charlotte, you know you have loved me all these months and marriage to me is what you long for.' Richard's voice was menacing.

'I have no desire to marry you,' I told him, my voice getting stronger at each word I spoke. 'You are correct that at one time I longed for you but that was before I got to know you.'

'But I am the same person,' Richard argued.

'Sometimes you are and sometimes you are like a completely different man,' I shouted at him.

'We will carry on with the ceremony,' Richard said to the priest, catching hold of my arm so tightly that it hurt.

'No we will not,' I told my employer

angrily, 'for if we do, then I shall tell Lina that you tried to marry me against my will.' At these words, Richard relaxed his hold on me and I freed myself from his grasp.

'Lina,' Richard uttered the name gently.

'Yes, Richard Roseby, your daughter. You know you adore her, for that is the only good thing about you. I realised long ago that you love only her.'

'I do indeed love her with my whole being. It has always been Lina and myself and she has brought me such joy.'

'Then think of her, for I would not willingly wish to upset her, or cause her to think ill of you,' I spoke to him as to a child. In the pause which followed, the priest spoke, 'If I am no longer needed, then I ask please that I leave,' he implored.

'Wait one moment,' Richard told him.

'And why did you see fit to drug my wine and bring me to this place to marry me under pretence, what possible motive could you have?' I had to ask the question, which now my head was clear, was the uppermost thought in my mind.

There was silence until Verity spoke. 'Richard has gambling debts and could lose Middlepark if it goes on much longer,' she said quietly.

'And you,' I pointed to her as I spoke, 'you, a gentlewoman, are in league with this, that Richard should marry an unwilling bride for money.'

'I am ashamed to say I am,' said Verity as she lowered her head, unable to look at me.

'Well I hope you've both come to your senses and be thankful that I shall say no more about it, but only for Lina's sake, because I have grown very fond of her.' My words, I realised, were true. I had become very attached to Lina over the past months and would not wish to hurt her or cause her any unhappiness and if she knew of this charade, what would she think of her father, who she adored. All was quiet, except for the priest snapping his Prayer Book shut. My head thumped and then the door burst open.

It was Jonathon, the mist swirling in with him. I ran to him and as he enfolded me gently in his arms, at last, I knew where I belonged. It had taken this to make me understand my true feelings.

'What is going on here?' Jonathon asked, as I snuggled closely against him, safe at last.

'How did you come to be here?' asked Richard.

'Ruby told her sister, who works at Redcliffe, that Miss Trent had gone out in this awful weather and I set out to look for her. I saw your pony and trap outside a deserted chapel. I came in to see what was happening,' he explained. 'What is a priest doing here and why the rose petals?' he said looking down. 'If I didn't know any different, I would think a marriage had taken place,' he observed.

'It very nearly did,' I said looking up at him, 'with a reluctant bride.'

'You cad, Roseby!' my beloved said angrily, stepping toward him, but I caught his arm to stop him.

'No, Jonathon, there is Lina to consider and fortuitously, the marriage didn't take place. Let us go, for I wish to go to bed and sleep, or my head will explode.'

'Very well, dear heart,' said Jonathon, still glaring at Richard, 'but be sure, Richard Roseby, that I shall not forget any of this for quite some time.'

'Nor I,' I whispered as we all dispersed into the mist, Jonathon taking me, reluctantly, back to Middlepark, but I knew that I would be safe now, for Richard would not wish to upset Lina.

★ ★ ★

That night, I slept well in spite of my ordeal at the deserted chapel. Next morning I had arranged to meet Jonathon after breakfast at the gates of

Middlepark. My head was clear and free of pain, for which I was thankful. I breakfasted with Lina and told her I had the day off, at which, she said she would spend the day with her father and Verity. Jonathon was waiting for me at the gates of Middlepark in his pony and trap. On seeing me, he jumped agilely to the ground and ran toward me, gathering me in his arms.

'Dear Charlotte, I have been so worried about you all night,' he said, putting me at arms length and looking me up and down.

'Worry no longer, Jonathon, for I am well, just a little tired,' I assured him, 'and I have every confidence that I am safe here, for I have been all these months before.'

'But yesterday,' my new found love uttered with passion in his voice, 'to be drugged and led to be married against your will, I know it is a crime.'

'But I am unscathed and I am certain that the drug was quite mild, for I came to my senses fairly quickly but, mixed with the wine, it was a little more potent than it should have been,' I told him.

'Now you are making excuses for your employer.'

'Please don't look at it like that,' I urged him, touching his cheek with my hand. 'Mr Roseby is obviously a worried man and in danger of losing all he has, so stupidly, he sought to solve the problem by marrying me and my money. In truth, I am quite worried for him, if only for Lina's sake.'

'What a charitable young woman I have fallen in love with,' was Jonathon's answer. 'But I still feel that a crime has been committed against the woman I love.'

'Then think of it no longer and let us go for a ride, for I wish to go to East Budleigh Church,' I urged him. When settled in the trap and bowling gently along the country lane, I explained to Jonathon about Madeline's letters and how I needed to find Joanna in the Family Bible.

'Why do you need to know?' was his question, but I found it hard to explain that I was now tangled up, inexplicably, in the mystery of Madeline and had to see it through to the end. There was also something niggling in my brain which I couldn't quite recall, something which was said in the chapel last night while my mind was hazy. Try as I might, I couldn't recall it.

'Can you stop here for a moment please, Jonathon?' I asked him suddenly and he quickly pulled the lovely brown pony to a halt.

'Do you feel unwell?' he asked, deep concern obvious in his voice.

'No,' I said smiling at him. 'I think we've just passed Holly Cottage.'

'Yes, indeed we have,' Jonathon replied, 'Miss Curtis' residence.'

'Then I need to see her, if she is in, please, for I feel the nurse could solve a lot of the mystery,' I told Jonathon who jumped down from the trap and assisted me to the ground, his hands lingering gently on my waist.

'I love you,' he said suddenly.

'And I you, but I have to solve this mystery before I can move forward,' I explained gently, the words of love bringing a tear to my eye, which Jonathon observed and he took a white handkerchief from his pocket and dabbed the tear away.

'Thank you,' I said, my heart bursting with love for him. 'Now let us see if Miss Curtis is home.' She was indeed at home and ushered us into her living-room. My first thought was how clean everything was, from the white walls to the scrubbed floor and woollen mats scattered around. There was a smell of baking drifting through the cottage and everything was so homely, I could have lived here myself.

'You've come here at last,' Miss Curtis said when we were all seated on comfortable chairs with silk cushions of a deep red.

'I need to ask you something, Miss Curtis, do you possibly know who Madeline was?' I began.

'Indeed I do, Miss Trent, for I am Anna,' she said softly.

'Then it was you who wrote messages on my mirror,' I gasped.

'Yes, I am the culprit, as I wanted Madeline's story to be told,' the nurse revealed. 'But that doesn't answer how you know about Madeline, Miss Trent. I just thought that being young, you would have pursued the two messages I left, especially my name, and I knew that we were bound to meet one day when I visited Lina, but alas you never asked any questions, so I had to ask you to come to me.'

At the nurse's admission, I told her how I had found Madeline's letters. As I related the story, Miss Curtis' eyes filled with tears. 'Poor Madeline, she loved him so,' Miss Curtis said.

'But who, Miss Curtis? Please tell me who it was she was in love with for I have tried to work it out for many weeks,' I pleaded an answer to the question that had haunted me for some time.

'You haven't worked it out, Miss Trent?' the nurse said. 'Well, it is young master Richard.'

'Richard Roseby.' I breathed a sigh of relief that at last I knew. 'So Lina is Madeline's daughter,' I said slowly, at last understanding dawning on me.

'Yes, Lina is Madeline and Richard's daughter.' As she spoke, Miss Curtis went across and looked from the window as she continued. 'Lina was born in this very cottage and her poor mother died two days later. I pleaded with Richard's father to allow Lina to be brought up in her rightful home. Master Richard wanted it too, for he was beside himself that he did not marry Madeline. His parents, especially his mother, would not hear of it. I said they should have eloped if Richard had an ounce of loyalty in him, but he would not thwart his mother, but I have to say, he has looked after Lina and brought her up on his own and above all, he loves her.' Here the nurse stopped, wrapped up, no doubt, in her memories of the past, which had indeed, come to the fore many years later.

'And where is Joanna?' I asked her, 'for you used to be her nurse.'

'Yes, indeed — and Madeline her governess,' Miss Curtis said, turning back from the window to look at me. 'It is Miss Verity, who is now at Middlepark.' The niggling thought of something said last night while at the chapel came to me. Last night, Verity had called Richard 'brother'.

'But why Verity, and not Joanna?' was my next question to Miss Curtis, who had now sat back down.

'Joanna was named Joanna Verity. When she was young, about eighteen, or so, she was accused of pushing her mother down the stairs at Middlepark, not long after Lina was born. Her mother died from a broken neck. Joanna and her mother had been heard to be arguing, not long before the accident, by a number of guests at Middlepark and one of the guests said he actually saw Joanna push Mrs Roseby, as he went in the hallway to collect his cape, but he was a short-sighted gentleman and his evidence was dismissed. It was quite a scandal at the time and Joanna was sent abroad where she married and she never returned to live in this country until her husband died a little over a year ago. Since she came back, she has used the name Verity and Lina does not know she is her aunt, but one day she will have to be told.' Here the nurse stopped.

'Told about her mother, too,' I said to no one of us in particular.

'That too,' said Miss Curtis with gusto. 'Now let us partake of a cup of tea.' While drinking tea and eating small sandwiches, Miss Curtis said, 'Have I solved all your mysteries for you now, Miss Trent?' at which words she smiled.

'No,' I said, 'there is one other. Who is the man in the miniature I found with the letters?'

'That would be Madeline's brother.

She adored him, but sadly, he died as a young man. She kept the miniature with her all the time.'

Her words had revealed all to me but there was one more question I had to ask.. 'Please can you tell me what Madeline looked like, Miss Curtis?'

'She was a lot like you, Miss Trent,' the nurse replied.

As we left the cottage, I looked back thinking of Madeline and her unhappy life, then I thought of Richard and the words came to me without conscious thought. 'You are a coward, Sir,' as indeed Richard Roseby is.

In spite of that, my employer had written those beautiful love letters and truly believed that he would never love anyone but Madeline, with this thought I felt some sympathy for him. In all of this, the one thing which mattered above all else, was the fact that he dearly loved his daughter. How I wished that Madeline knew this. I would never know if I had seen Madeline's apparition in the mirror in my room at Middlepark for I was then a daydreamer, but I am pleased I learned her story.

Jonathon and I went into the church as I wished to sit for a while and think over all Miss Curtis had told us that day. As we neared the church path, I looked up at the tall square tower and thought what a lovely place this would be to marry. No one had asked me yet, but I had a strong feeling that Jonathon would ask me one day.

★ ★ ★

I stayed at Middlepark until the following Spring, wishing to do right by Lina and not desert her until she was ready for me to leave. The young man, Brett, whom she had danced with at the ball, courted her and in the March, they became betrothed it was then I knew it was time to leave Middlepark.

'Lina,' I said to her one day when we were sat together stitching her trousseau in the drawing room.

'I know what you are going to say,' Lina said, raising her head from her work to look at me.

'Then I have no need to say it,' I teased her, as I always did for we were friends more than companion and charge now.

'No, Charlotte, please speak to me. Do not tease,' she said seriously.

'You know that the time has come for me to leave. You are a woman now and no longer in need of a companion,' I told her, as gently as I could.

'You are right, Charlotte. You need to pursue your own life with Mr Moor, as much as you loathe Georgina.' Here she giggled for we were always talking of Jonathon's sister although I had learned over the past months to tolerate her.

'I am pleased you understand,' I said with relief, for I had picked my moment well.

I saw little of Richard Roseby or his sister Verity except at dinner when I joined then as usual. I felt their problems must have resolved themselves somehow, for we were all still at Middlepark and Richard seemed more relaxed these days. I could never forgive him or Verity for trying to force me into a marriage on that misty evening in September, but as I told Jonathon, I stayed for Lina's sake.

I had declined Mrs Rivers' offer of employment, but had agreed, on special occasions, to sketch a gown for her, to which suggestion she gratefully agreed.

As Jonathon and I walked through the grounds of Redcliffe Manor, admiring the Spring flowers, we found ourselves by the lake. 'I need to speak with you' said Jonathon stopping and turning me to him 'and this is the very place to do it.'

'It is our place, isn't it,' I said. 'Our very special place, because this is where it all began.'

'It is indeed, Charlotte and that is why I want to ask you here, in our special place, if you will make me the happiest of men and marry me'?

'Yes, yes, yes,' I told him, my joy unconfined and I reached up to kiss him gently on the mouth. 'Together we will bring this glorious house to its former glory,' I told him.

'You said that one day you would describe Redcliffe Manor to me in a word,' Jonathon said. As we stood, our arms around each other, full of love for one another, I looked down toward the hauntingly beautiful home I would share with Jonathon for the rest of our lives, a place where we would love and laugh and hopefully raise a family. I looked up at the man I loved.

'It is a jewel,' I told him. 'A precious jewel for us both to treasure.'

THE END